The Happy Hollisters and the Mystery of the Midnight Trolls

By JERRY WEST

Illustrated by Helen S. Hamilton

GARDEN CITY, NEW YORK

DOUBLEDAY & COMPANY, INC.

The author gratefully acknowledges the assistance given to him by Mrs. Robert P. Guenther, Supervisor, Materials and Textbook Center, New Jersey Commission for the Blind.

Contents

1. The Lost Letter 5
2. Learning a Code 14
3. Post Office Surprise 25
4. A Piggy Turnover 35
5. A New Friend 45
6. Pamela Johnsdottir 58
7. Setting a Trap 66
8. Tricky Trolls 75
9. Snaefell Stikki 83
10. The Magic Whale 94
11. Teakettle Island 103
12. Shinbone Secrets 115
13. The Skilligan 126
14. Pinpoint Messages 136
15. The Ski Lodge Ghost 145
16. The Copter Captive 153
17. The Thingvellir Spy 163
18. A Spooky Catch 175

BRAILLE

CELL OF SIX DOTS

A B C D E F G H I

J K L M N O P Q R

S T U V W X Y Z

CHAPTER 1

The Lost Letter

"HERE comes Daddy's sailplane," shouted Ricky Hollister as he ran across the lawn.

"Where?" his six-year-old sister Holly asked, looking up into the blue summer sky.

"Not there, silly," said red-headed Ricky, who was seven. "It's coming down the road!"

"Oh," said Holly and raced after him, her pigtails flying.

The Hollister house stood between Pine Lake and Shoreham Road. Ricky and Holly reached the curb to see a pickup truck pulling a boat trailer.

On it was a long airplane fuselage, and inside the truck were the two wings. Several neighborhood children skipped behind as the load turned into the driveway.

"I'm going to fly in it when the wings are on," Holly said.

"Oh boy, it's really neat!" called out twelve-year-old Dave Mead. He added, "Hey, where are the rest of the kids?"

There were three more Hollister children. Pete, the oldest, was twelve, and Pam, ten, was next in line. They had gone on a bicycle errand for their mother. Little Sue was the youngest. The four-year-old had been inside playing with her dolls but at that moment she flung open the front screen door to scamper out as fast as her chubby legs would carry her.

As she reached the truck, down stepped Mr. Hollister, tall, broad-shouldered and grinning like a boy. He was followed by Indy Roades, who helped him in the Trading Post. This was a hardware, toy and sports shop in downtown Shoreham.

The children's father was a flying enthusiast and had built a sailplane himself in the huge garage behind his store. Now he was going to assemble it on his property.

Sue leaped up into his arms. Following her was Mrs. Hollister, a pert and pretty woman.

"Oh, John!" she said. "I didn't know your plane was so big!"

Just then bicycle tires squealed, and Pete and Pam zoomed into the driveway. Pete was a sturdy boy with blond hair and clear blue eyes. Pam had fluffy golden hair, which blew about in the breeze as she skidded to a halt and stepped off her bicycle.

Smiling, they joined the excited youngsters watching the men pull the fuselage onto the lawn beside the garage. Then Pete and his friend Dave helped to carry the wings and lay them down on either side of the fuselage.

"Is your father really going to fly that glider without an engine?" seven-year-old Donna Martin asked.

"Sure," Ricky said. "He's a good flyer!"

Just then a boy a little larger than Pete strode by, his hands thrust deep in his pockets. Joey Brill was Pete's age and a classmate. But instead of a smile, he wore a frown. "What's going on here?" he demanded.

"Daddy's sailplane is ready," Pam said.

"You mean glider."

"No. The real name is sailplane," Pam replied. "But lots of people call them gliders."

"He made it himself," Pete stated proudly.

"Our father is an inventor too," Ricky bragged, watching the men attach the wings.

Joey sniffed and walked around the plane, looking at it from every angle. "I'd say this thing can't fly at all," he proclaimed.

"Of course it will," said Pete. "And I'm going up with Dad too!"

"You think your father's great, don't you?" taunted Joey.

"Of course."

"My father can do more things than yours."

"So what?" said Pete and walked away.

Before Joey could think of any more mean things

7

to say, the mailman came along the sidewalk, waving a fistful of letters toward the Hollisters.

Pam raced over to get them. "Hello, Mr. Barnes. They're all for us?"

"Every one of 'em, young lady."

Pam thanked him and read the envelopes as she walked toward her mother. A big brown one, postmarked Froston, Canada, was addressed to the Happy Hollister Children.

"Something from Gram!" Pam cried out joyfully.

With the other children looking on, she pulled out a piece of heavy paper. On it were small dots arranged in an odd pattern.

"Yikes!" Ricky exclaimed. "Grandma has sent us a funny message."

"A bumpy code," Holly giggled, pulling on one of her pigtails.

Mrs. Hollister told her children that this was Braille, the kind of writing used by blind people.

"Oh," Pam cried out. "Is Grandma—"

"No, there's nothing wrong with Grandma," her mother assured her and explained that Gram had been working for some time preparing Braille books for the blind in Canada. She and Gramp Hollister lived there in retirement.

"She has a special machine that types Braille," Mrs. Hollister said.

"Can I see it?" Ricky asked and took the sheet to show it around to his friends.

"It's my grandmother's secret code," he said importantly.

Joey Brill edged up, and before anyone could stop him, he grabbed the Braille letter.

"Let me figure out the code," he said. "I'll bet it's easy."

"Hey! Give it back!" Ricky shouted, but the bully scooted off, turning only briefly to stick out his tongue.

Ricky raced after him. Then Pete, Pam and Dave hurried to the street, but by the time they looked up and down, Joey was nowhere to be seen.

"Where'd he go, Ricky?" Pam called out to her brother, who stood dejectedly two blocks away.

"I don't know. He disappeared between those houses."

"Joey's just terrible," Dave said angrily.

"Don't worry," Pam replied. "His mother will make him give the letter back."

"I'll go over to his house right away," Pete volunteered. "Want to come, Pam?"

"Okay."

The Brills lived nearby and the Hollisters reached their home in a few minutes. Joey was on the front porch, rocking back and forth in a chair.

"What do you want?" he asked rudely.

"To see your mother!" Pam declared.

"She's not home."

Hearing the voices, Mrs. Brill appeared at the

"Hey! Give it back!" Ricky shouted.

door, her hands white with flour. "Oh dear, are you children fighting again? What is it now?"

"Joey took a letter our grandmother sent to us," Pete said, "and we want it back."

"Aw, I didn't take any letter!" Joey said.

"It wasn't exactly a written letter," Pam explained. "It was in Braille."

"For blind people?"

"Yes."

"Why, there's nobody blind in your house," Mrs. Brill said loftily. "So how could my Joey have taken your letter?"

"But it was written by our grandmother," Pam went on stoutly. "She helps blind people."

Mrs. Brill wiped her hands on her apron and looked at Joey. "Give back the letter!" she ordered.

"I don't have it."

Tears came to Pam's eyes. "Mrs. Brill," she said, "he's lying. We saw him take it."

The woman eyed her son sternly. "Give back the letter, I said!" As she moved toward him, Joey cringed.

"I—I don't have it now!"

"Then where is it?"

Joey said he had tucked it into his shirt, but as he ran home it fell out and was lost.

Disappointed, the children turned and left, wondering whether there was an important secret in the lost letter. What had their grandmother written? Did it require an urgent reply?

When they reached home, they were surprised to see a newspaper photographer taking pictures of the sailplane. Their father was talking to a reporter.

"I plan to take part in several soaring meets," he said and explained that he would give his two-seater a tryout soon.

At supper the Hollisters talked over the day's events. The sailplane was good news, but Gram's letter was not. They must write and tell her of the loss. After they had finished eating dessert Mr. Hollister said, "Come on, boys. We'll have to tie down the plane for the night."

Ricky wrinkled his nose and scratched his head. "So it won't fly away?"

"If there happens to be a strong wind it would lift up like a kite," his father said. He explained that they would have to tie ropes around the wings and attach them to pegs, driven into the ground.

After this had been done, Pam called Zip, their collie dog. He came bounding up and licked her hand. "Down, boy," she said and attached a long leash to his collar. She tied the other end to a tree.

"Zip can stand on guard just in case," Pam said.

As dusk settled down over the shore of Pine Lake, Ricky, Holly and Sue chased fireflies around the house and put them in a glass jar.

Finally Mrs. Hollister called her children inside. "Time for bed," she said.

Ricky punched holes in the tin lid and screwed it at the top of the jar.

"May I take these into my bedroom?" he asked.

"All right," his mother replied, "but let those poor little things free in the morning."

Just before Pete went upstairs Zip started barking wildly. The boy dashed out onto the lawn.

"Quiet! Quiet, Zip!" he commanded.

The collie stopped barking. Instead he whined and growled.

Pete looked around. He could see nobody. All of a sudden he heard a rustle. Then, as his eyes became used to the darkness, he spied a small, bent-over man hastening out of the driveway!

"What do you want? Wait!" Pete shouted and set off after the intruder. By the time the boy reached the sidewalk, however, the stranger had vanished.

From the porch, Mr. Hollister called to his son. "Who is it?"

"Don't know, Dad. I'm looking around." Pete peered into the dark bushes bordering the walk and listened.

Then something touched his leg slightly, and he cried out in fright!

CHAPTER 2

Learning a Code

PETE stood terrified, afraid to look around at the thing running up his leg. If it was a snake, it might bite him at any second.

The boy was about to slap at it, when a voice behind him said, "Don't be afraid!"

With knees shaking, Pete turned his head slowly to look over his shoulder. He faced a thin, stooped man with strange, unblinking eyes. In his hand he held a white stick, with which he tapped against Pete's leg.

The boy still was so frightened that he could not get a word out of his mouth.

The man asked, "Are you one of the Hollisters?"

"Yes, I'm Pete." He managed a smile. "You nearly scared the wits out of me. Did you run out of our yard?"

"Yes. Please take me to your house, Pete," the stranger continued, "and don't let your dog bite me. You go ahead, I'll follow."

Pete thought about it for a moment. The man looked kind. "Okay," he said.

Pete turned and walked along the driveway slowly. Behind him came the man, tapping with his cane.

Suddenly it dawned on Pete that the stranger must be blind. He stopped and said, "Could I take you by the arm, sir?"

"No—no. Just go on, sonny. I can follow all right."

Mr. and Mrs. Hollister were standing on the porch.

"Mother, Dad, this man wants to see you," Pete said and led the visitor into the living room.

"How do you do?" Mrs. Hollister said kindly, sizing up the situation at once.

The children's father introduced himself and offered the stranger a seat.

As the blind man felt for a chair with his cane he said, "My name is Kovac. I have something which belongs to you."

He found the sofa and sat down, at the same time reaching into his jacket and pulling out a Braille message.

"Well, for goodness sake!" Mrs. Hollister exclaimed. "That looks like the letter our children lost!"

"Sure." Pete nodded. "That's the one all right."

15

"Oh, thank you so much," Pam said. "How did you know it belonged to us?"

Mr. Kovac smiled. "It is addressed to the Happy Hollister Children. Would you like me to read the letter to you?"

"Yes! Please!" Pam said. "It's from our grandmother."

The man's fingers flitted over the letter. " 'Dear Children,' " he began. " 'Gram is writing to you in code. It is Braille. How would you like to visit me and meet a special friend? Also, I wish you could solve the mystery of the midnight trolls. With love, Gram.' "

"That's it," Mr. Kovac said.

Meanwhile, three figures in their nighties had appeared at the top of the steps and gradually stepped down like quiet little mice.

All of a sudden Sue's voice chirped, "I know what a troll is! That's when you pay money to cross a bridge."

Mr. Kovac turned to the source of the sound and smiled. "So there are five Happy Hollister children."

Pam looked in wonderment. "You only heard three of us, Mr. Kovac."

"I heard the other two creeping down the stairs," he replied.

Introductions were quickly made and the younger children shook hands with the blind man.

Holly spoke up. "But you didn't tell us how you got the letter which Joey Brill swiped."

Before Mr. Kovac could answer, Mrs. Hollister whispered to Pam, "Put on a kettle, dear, and make a cup of tea for our guest."

"I didn't really find the letter," Mr. Kovac said. "Somebody else did—a young woman. I can't remember her name, but she knows I am blind and brought it to me."

"How did you find out where we lived?" asked Pam.

Mr. Kovac smiled and clasped his hands on top of the cane which he held between his knees. "I only moved to Shoreham a little while ago," he said, "but I've already heard about the Hollister family."

He told them that he lived in a little house about a quarter of a mile from the Hollister home. Soon the sound of the whistling teakettle beckoned Pam into the kitchen. She asked Holly to set the table.

The pig-tailed girl brought two hostess tables into the living room and Pam poured tea for the grown-ups. Then she offered a plate of cookies to Mr. Kovac. He placed his cane on the floor beside his chair and helped himself.

"Thank you so much," he said. As he sipped his tea, Mrs. Hollister told about Gram and the work she did to help the blind.

"That's very kind of her," Mr. Kovac said.

"I'd like to help blind people too," Pam spoke up. "Is Braille hard to learn?"

"Not at all for bright young people," their guest replied and invited Pam to visit his apartment with her brothers and sisters.

He left shortly afterward with the thanks of the Hollisters still ringing in his ears. But the children's father would not let him walk and insisted on driving him home. When Mr. Hollister returned, the living room was full of laughter as his youngsters were discussing trolls.

"A toll, t-o-l-l, is when you pay to go over a bridge," Pam told Sue.

"Well, it sounds like a troll," Sue said, then added with a giggle, "do trolls pay tolls?"

But Pam was not listening to her joke. She had pulled several encyclopedias from a shelf and was sprawled on the floor leafing through them. "Here," she said and pushed one book over to Sue. "These are trolls. Look at them!"

While Sue, Holly and Ricky chuckled over pictures of funny little dwarfs with cute clothes and pointed hats, Pam looked up Braille.

"Listen to this, Pete," she said and read aloud:

"'Louis Braille, a fifteen-year-old French blind student developed a raised dot-dash reading system in 1824, which is based on a cell of six dots. From the sixty-three possible arrangements of the dots, he worked out an alphabet, punctuation marks and numerals. A blind person reads by running his fingers along the dots. He can write on a six-key machine called a Braille writer.'"

"That's what your grandmother uses," Mrs. Hollister put in. "And I'm sure you can learn to use one too, Pam."

When they had finished with the books, more questions poured from the children. Could they please visit Gram and Gramp in Canada?

"Perhaps," Mrs. Hollister said. "Don't forget Daddy has to fly his sailplane."

"We could go alone," Pete suggested.

"Sure, and solve the mystery of the midnight trolls," Pam added. "I wonder what they do at midnight?"

"We'll see," Mrs. Hollister said. "Now it's time for all of you to go to bed."

"I want to dream about trolls," said Ricky.

"And I want to be one," added Sue as she crept slowly up the stairway to her room.

"You're one already," Ricky teased. "All you need is a pointed hat."

At breakfast next morning the younger children again begged to visit their grandparents.

"We'll have to wait until Daddy tests the sailplane," Pete said.

Mr. Hollister had told them that he would be flying in a New York state competition in a few days, and if possible, in the big international sailplane meet in Iceland.

"That's a Scandinavian country," Pam mused. "Do you suppose they have trolls up there?"

Holly hunched up her shoulders and made a pig-tail mustache. This made Sue laugh and dribble a spoonful of cereal down the front of her dress.

"Now look what you've done!" Pam said as she wiped off the food with a napkin. Then she added, "Come on, girls, I have an idea. Let's visit Mr. Kovac."

"Goody," Holly said.

While the two boys stayed with their father to look over the new sailplane, the three sisters held hands and skipped along the sidewalk in the direction of Mr. Kovac's little house.

They found him sitting in the sun on a tiny patch of lawn beside the front door. He heard them coming, and before they could say anything, called out, "What a nice early visit from the Happy Hollisters!"

"We've come to learn Braille," Pam said.

"Good. Wait a minute."

Mr. Kovac went inside and returned with a card table which he set up in the sunshine. Then he brought out a Braille printing machine and sheets of heavy paper.

Pam helped him to get three folding chairs, and the children sat down for their lesson.

The Braille writer looked just like a typewriter but only had six keys. Mr. Kovac inserted a paper in the back and then pressed the keys hard.

"I'm going to write the alphabet for you," he said.

Punch, punch, punch, punch! Now the sheet had lots of little dots on it.

"You see these two parallel rows of three dots each?" Mr. Kovac asked. "All our letters are made from them." He proceeded to show them that *a* was dot number one. *B* was one and two, *c* was one and four, *d* was one, four and five, *e* one and five, and so on.

Pam paid strict attention. After they had studied the strange alphabet for a while, she said, "Mr. Kovac, will you help us write a letter to our grandmother?"

"Of course. What would you like to say?" He ran a fresh piece of paper in the Braille writer and Pam dictated:

"Dear Gram: Thanks for your Braille letter. We'll try to visit you and meet your special friend. Right now we are taking lessons in Braille from Mr. Kovac. Love from all of us. Pam."

Mr. Kovac went into the house and brought out a brown envelope. "You certainly learned a lot today," he said, as Pam wrote the address, "and such good students too!"

When the card table and chairs were put away,

Mr. Kovac pressed the keys hard.

the children thanked the blind man and started for home. He accompanied them up the street for a way. Suddenly he made a strange clicking sound with his tongue and tapped with his toes.

Holly laughed. "I didn't know you were in show business, Mr. Kovac."

"Oh, I'm not. I really shouldn't be doing this."

"Why not?"

The blind man explained that the sounds he made with his tongue and the toes of his shoes sent little noises ahead. They bounced off whatever was in front of him and came back to warn him that something was in his way.

"Do all blind people do that?" Holly asked.

"Only a few," Mr. Kovac said with a shrug. "I really should use my radar sight."

Pam's eyes widened. "You mean you have a built-in radar?"

"Of course. Everybody does," Mr. Kovac said as he paused before skirting a tree which extended partly into the sidewalk. He explained that if a person walked along with his eyes closed, certain vibrations in the air would touch his face and warn him of an obstacle.

"Oh, that's wonderful," Pam said. "We'll have to try that sometime."

After thanking their host, they ran down the street. At the first postbox, they mailed the letter. When they reached home, they found their father and Pete sitting in the sailplane. Mr. Hollister was manipulating the controls.

"Everything is in great shape, Pete," he said. "I can't wait to fly her."

Just then Mrs. Hollister called everyone in for lunch. During the meal Pam told about the letter to her grandmother and what they had learned at Mr. Kovac's place. For the rest of the day excitement ran high until every light had been turned off in the Hollisters' home.

About midnight everything was quiet. Suddenly there was a loud *bang*. Mrs. Hollister jumped up. "John!" she called to her husband, "that noise came from Holly's room!"

CHAPTER 3

Post Office Surprise

BEFORE Mrs. Hollister's feet found the slippers at the side of her bed, she heard a loud wailing. Now everyone jumped out of their beds and dashed into Holly's room. Lights were switched on.

Holly stood next to the wall holding her forehead and crying.

"What happened?" Pam asked.

"Looks as if she banged her head," Pete observed.

Mrs. Hollister put her arms around the little girl's shoulders. "Did you fall out of bed?"

Holly continued to blubber for a few seconds more, then she wiped her tears with the back of her hand and sobbed, "My radar doesn't work!"

"Your radar?" her mother said. "What on earth—"

"Oh, I know," said Pam, bobbing her head up and down. "She was testing out the radar that blind people use. Isn't that right, Holly?"

"Yes," her sister sniffled. "I woke up dreaming about it. But mine doesn't work!"

"It just can't be learned overnight," her mother said. "Come on, sit down on the bed, Holly."

"Yikes, you must have smashed into that wall pretty hard," Ricky stated, peering closely at the bump on his sister's forehead.

Pam hastened to the bathroom and returned with a cloth sopping with cold water. "Here, put this on, honey," she said to Holly.

Then she went into her room, opened a dresser drawer and rummaged beneath some blouses. She pulled out one of her treasures. It was a small rubber ball attached to an elastic string. Pam liked to tie the string around her finger and bounce the ball. Now she brought it to her sister.

"Here, Holly, take this. It'll make up for your bump," she said kindly and gave her the toy.

Holly stopped sniffling and broke into a big smile. "Oh, thank you, Pam," she said. "I'll be very careful with it."

Next day Mr. Hollister set off early to the Trading Post, but returned in midmorning with Indy Roades. With the help of the two boys, they disassembled the sailplane. The wings were put into the truck, and the fuselage lifted onto the trailer.

Joey Brill stood at the side of the road watching but did not venture on the Hollisters' property.

"I'm going to take her up for the first test," Mr. Hollister told his family.

"Do be careful, John, won't you?" his wife warned.

"Oh, don't worry about Daddy," Ricky piped up. "He's a good flyer."

Mr. Hollister said he would take the two boys with him. "Once I learn how to operate this bird," he said, "you can all come up to the State Park and watch me."

Ricky and Pete got into the truck, settled themselves beside the wings and waved as they left the driveway.

Joey made a rude noise with his mouth, and Ricky replied by sticking thumbs in his ears and wagging his fingers at the bully.

Pete chuckled. "Oh, don't even bother with that goof," he said.

Thirty minutes later, the truck pulled into a small airport in the State Park. Mr. Hollister assembled his sailplane near the landing strip. When he was all ready, a car drove up with a nylon rope attached to its back. Mr. Hollister took it and hitched it to the front of the sailplane on a movable hook.

"Look, I'm going up alone the first time," he said to the boys. "I'll give you a ride later."

Mr. Hollister secured himself in the cockpit.

The two looked on, awe-struck, as the car moved far ahead of the plane and the nylon rope was paid out. When it became taut, he waved to his sons and gave a signal. The car started racing down the runway, gathering speed. As it did, the sailplane became air-borne. It rose higher and higher into the sky.

Ricky shouted and jumped up and down. He called out words of encouragement to his father. Finally Mr. Hollister pulled a lever, releasing the cable tow. Now he was soaring along, quietly, seeking out updrafts of air currents to carry his shiny bird even higher.

The plane soared among the fluffy white clouds, banked and after a while started its descent to the airfield. Ten minutes later it came to a perfect landing on the green grass beside the runway.

The boys raced over to congratulate their father. "Dad, it was great! Perfect!" Pete said.

Ricky wrinkled his freckled nose, looked up at Mr. Hollister and pulled on his arm. "You can do things better than Joey's father any time!" he said.

"Now will you take me up, Dad?" Pete asked. "Can I sit at the dual controls behind you?"

"All right," Mr. Hollister nodded and glanced at Ricky. "Your turn will be next."

"Well, eh—maybe not today," Ricky said and added quickly, "There isn't any motor in this, is there, Dad?"

"You're not chicken, are you, Ricky?" Pete asked.

"Course not. Go ahead. You take a ride."

The tow car was summoned and Pete wriggled into the seat behind his father. His heart thumped, and there was a funny feeling in the pit of his stomach.

Pete swallowed a couple of times as the tow car raced along the runway. They were in motion! Next they were off the ground heading into the air at a steep angle.

"Crickets!" Pete said, catching his breath.

When the towline was released, the plane leveled off. Mr. Hollister glanced out through the canopy then at his son. In the majestic silence of the air, they grinned at each other.

"Nothing like it, is there, Pete?"

"Dad! This is keen. Hey! Watch out!"

Pete looked up to see a single engine airplane above them. It was about thirty feet to the right.

Mr. Hollister saw it too. He banked sharply to the left. The sailplane sideslipped, knifing toward the ground below. After a few tense seconds he righted it and headed over the treetops toward the airport.

Would they make it? Pete saw the tops of the green trees come closer and closer toward the fuselage. The grassy strip of the runway looked so far away!

The sailplane banked sharply.

He leaned forward in his seat as if to urge the sailplane over the obstacles, which now loomed larger in its path. Finally they passed the last clump of trees, whose topmost leafy branches scraped like fingers at the bottom of the fuselage. Then they were in the clearing. The plane landed like a feather on the grass.

"Phew!" Mr. Hollister looked at Pete with relief. "Thanks for the warning, son. The other craft should have seen us. It might have come down right on top of us if you hadn't yelled."

Shortly afterward the sailplane was towed to a hangar beside the runway, where it was to remain until the day of the big meet. Pete and Mr. Hollister went back to where they had left Ricky.

"Yikes, that was a neat trick!" the redhead called out as he raced up to them.

Pete just looked at his father and winked. The trio returned home and found nobody in. Apparently Mrs. Hollister had gone shopping with her daughters. Stuck in the door was a notice from the post office, saying that two packages were waiting there.

A little later Mrs. Hollister and the girls came back. Pam carried a large cakebox full of apple turnovers fresh from the bakery. At lunch stories were exchanged about the sailplane ride. Then Mrs. Hollister said, "You know there must be some mistake about this post office notice."

"Why, Mother?" Pam asked.

"Because I expect only one package. I sent my wrist watch to New York for repairs. It must have arrived."

Pete licked a piece of apple from his finger and said, "Maybe someone is sending you a surprise!"

"Holly and I'll get it," Ricky volunteered.

"Fine. If there really is a second package, just bring it home too."

Ricky took his bicycle giving his sister a ride on the back. Quickly he pedaled to the business section of town where the post office was located.

After presenting their notice at one of the windows, the clerk gave the children a small box.

"That must be Mother's wrist watch," Holly said.

"Isn't there a second package for us, though?" Ricky inquired.

The man looked on the counter. "Sure is. A big one too." He had to open an adjoining door to push the box out into the lobby. It was a heavy square carton, just about as large as the mails would allow and was marked fragile. The sender was Karl Sveinsson, of Reykjavik, Iceland.

"Crickets!" Ricky said. "How are we going to get this home?"

At that moment Holly spied a dark-haired boy pulling his coaster wagon past the front of the post office. He was Ricky's friend, eight-year-old Jeff Hunter.

"Jeff! Jeff!" she called out, running through the door. "Can we borrow your coaster wagon to cart a package home?"

"Sure," Jeff said.

Together with Ricky, he carried the carton outside and placed it in the wagon. Jeff had something else to do, and said he would pick up his wagon later at the Hollister home.

Ricky got a stout cord from the postal clerk and tied one end to the back of his bicycle and the other to the shaft of the wagon. Then he set off down the street, with Holly protecting the rear.

He was careful to pause briefly at every intersection, making sure that nothing came between his bicycle and the coaster wagon. As he crossed Fourth Avenue he suddenly heard the accelerating sound of a motorcycle.

Ricky saw the machine speeding in their direction. But the helmeted driver did not have his eyes on the road. Instead, he had turned his head to wave at a friend on the sidewalk.

The boy stopped. Should he retreat or hurry across in front of the motorcycle? *Oh, if he'd only look ahead!* Ricky thought in desperation.

But the cyclist merely smiled broadly and kept his eyes to the side of the street. He failed to see the Hollisters or the cord stretching between the bike and the wagon.

He ran over it, jerking the bicycle and wagon. Ricky flew over the handle bars and crashed to the ground. The box was flung onto the street and skidded along the curb.

Holly shrieked in fright and ran to her brother. "Ricky! Ricky! Are you hurt?" she cried.

CHAPTER 4

A Piggy Turnover

PEOPLE passing by rushed to the aid of Ricky Hollister. His knees and hands were scraped, but otherwise he was unhurt. He got up from the pavement and picked up his bicycle. It was not damaged. Then a frightened look came into his eyes. He turned to Holly. "Where's the box? What happened to it?"

Holly had been so concerned with Ricky's tumble that for the moment she had forgotten all about their important cargo. Now she gazed around.

The coaster wagon lay on its side near the curb. But the post office parcel, which had skidded down the street, was nowhere in sight!

Brushing off the attention of the passers-by, Ricky let go of the bike and dashed about wildly in search of the lost package. Holly righted the coaster wagon, pulled it to the curb, then joined her brother. Ricky kept asking people, "Did anybody see the parcel that was in our wagon?"

"What did it look like?" asked a tall woman in

35

a white hat. When the boy described it, she said, "I saw a man going around the corner with a big package like that."

Ricky jumped on his bike and pedaled off in the direction the woman had given, with Holly racing behind, pulling the wagon. Far down the street they saw a man. He was carrying their package!

Ricky caught up with him and said, "Wait a minute, mister. That's *our* package!"

The man paid no attention to him. He was short, squat and had a square jaw and deep lines in his face.

Now Holly reached them too. "Please put it right in our wagon. We have to take it home to daddy!" she said brightly.

The stranger stopped and scowled at the children. "I found this carton in the street," he said, "and want a reward for it!"

The youngsters noticed that he had a curious accent.

"A reward?" Ricky asked. Then he had a thought. Perhaps if he gave the man something there would be no more trouble, and he could take the parcel home to his father. He reached into his pocket and felt three coins.

Quickly he pulled out a dime and two nickels and offered them up on the palm of his hand. "Okay. Here's your reward. Now give us our package."

The stranger looked at the money and his lips curled. "Twenty cents! I want twenty dollars, or maybe even two hundred, if this package is valuable! Now get out of my way!"

Holly put her hands on her hips and her face got red. "You're horrid!" she said. "And besides, you can't fool around with U.S. mails!"

"That's right!" Ricky said. "The FBI will get after you!"

"Oh, really?" the man sneered. "This is not the U.S. mails. It comes from Iceland."

The two children did not know what to say to this, but as the stranger walked off, they tagged after him. Suddenly a police car appeared from around the corner. Ricky thought, "Oh, if it's only Officer Cal!"

Cal Newberry was a friendly young policeman who had helped the Hollisters on many of their mysteries. Occasionally they had helped him too.

Ricky poked Holly and pointed to the squad car. As it drew closer, the girl cried out. "Officer Cal, help! Help!" When the unpleasant stranger heard this, he looked startled and began walking at a faster clip.

He did not get far however. Officer Cal stopped the car and jumped out. "What's the trouble, kids?" he asked.

Holly pointed to the man and dragged the policeman along, quickly telling him what happened.

"Let's see the package!" Officer Cal demanded.

"I found it on the street and was going to return it to its owner," the man said.

"These are the Hollister children. Why didn't you give it to them?"

"I didn't know who they were!"

Officer Cal looked at the stranger with a steady gaze as he handed the box over without a word. Then he hastened away.

"Come on, I'll take you home," Officer Cal said to the children. "We'll put the package, the coaster wagon and the bike in the back of the car."

When this was done, Ricky and Holly slipped into the front seat beside the policeman. He picked up his microphone. "Taking Holly and Ricky Hollister home. No emergency."

By the time they pulled into the Hollister driveway, their father had already arrived from the Trading Post. He and Pete came out to greet Officer Cal. When his youngsters handed him the package, he looked at it in surprise.

"From Karl Sveinsson in Iceland!" he said.

"You know him, Daddy?" asked Pete.

"Yes, I've been corresponding with him on a revolutionary new invention. We think it's perfected."

"For a sailplane?"

"You're close, Pete," his father said. "It's a sailplane motor."

"But Dad—"

"Let's see what this is," Mr. Hollister went on and opened the package. The contents was packed tightly in excelsior. He reached his hand in, and amid the "ohs" and "ahs" of his children, pulled out a sleek sailplane model.

"Look at that!" Officer Cal said. "It's a beauty!"

Just then, the radio in the police car squawked and Officer Cal had to say good-by.

The youngsters followed their father into the living room where he put the little glider on the coffee table. It looked almost like his own sailplane, except for one thing. There was a ring around the narrowing fuselage near the tail, and a two-blade propeller was attached to the ring.

Pete noticed it and was perplexed. "But Dad," he said. "I thought gliders didn't have any motors!"

Mr. Hollister explained that some sailplanes had a small motor so that they would not have to be towed for take off. Also, it would come in handy in the event of an emergency.

"It's about the size of a VW engine," he said, "and can be popped out of the topside of the fuselage. A small propeller will assist the pilot in case he loses the updraft."

"But this propeller is placed altogether different," Pam observed.

"That's right. Mr. Sveinsson and I think that it's a great improvement."

"You mean, Dad, it will spin around the axis at the rear of the fuselage?" Pete asked.

"Exactly."

Mr. Hollister said that the Icelander and his brother-in-law who lived in Canada, had worked long and hard to perfect this idea.

"If you go to the international glider meet," Pam said, "perhaps you can talk to Mr. Sveinsson."

Mr. Hollister grinned boyishly. "That's what I've been looking forward to, Pam."

In the evening the Hollisters received a telephone call from Gram. She urged that the children come visit her right away. "Put them on a bus," she told Mrs. Hollister. "This way you can go to Iceland with John."

When the children heard this, they laughed in delight. Ricky even did a handspring and nearly knocked over a vase of flowers on an end table.

Their parents talked quietly together for a few minutes. Finally Mrs. Hollister said, "All right, you can pack tonight and start tomorrow. Scoot!"

"And, Pam, you must promise to keep a good eye on Sue," Mr. Hollister added.

"Of course, Daddy."

Packing did not take long, since the children were used to setting off on short notice. They knew the bus was to leave the depot in Shoreham early in the morning and could hardly go to sleep with sheer excitement.

Next day Pam was the first to get dressed and hurried downstairs. She wanted to make sure that White Nose, their cat, and the five kittens had their milk before she left. Then she filled Zip's bowl and patted the collie. "Take care of everything until we get back," she whispered in his ear, "and mind what Indy tells you."

Right after breakfast they left. The streets were quiet as Mr. Hollister drove his brood to the depot. As they boarded the bus, the driver chatted smilingly with their parents. "Leave the driving to us," he said with a pleasant chuckle, "and they'll all be safe in Froston tonight."

Then with a roar the bus moved out of the terminal and was on its way!

It had started out just a quarter full, but after stopping at several towns along the way, only a few seats were left vacant. The restless youngsters climbed in and out of these, and played other games to pass the time. Pam gave the younger trio pieces of paper on which they wrote the state license plates of passing cars. Then Holly took out her rubber ball and began bouncing it in the aisle.

The lunch stop was fun. Pete, who had the money, ordered hot dogs, hamburgers and drinks. Outside of Ricky's getting mustard on his nose, all went well. Then, in the middle of the afternoon, as they zoomed along a hilly highway that wound through a forest, the driver suddenly jammed on his brakes.

"Oh, oh," Pete said. "There's trouble ahead!"

Several other cars had slowed to a crawl. As the bus inched around a sharp curve, the youngsters gasped. There, beside the road, lay a small overturned truck. Its load of pigs was scrambling all over the highway and up steep sides sloping into the woods.

"Let's go and see what happened!" Ricky cried. The driver apparently had the same idea, because he swung the door open and several passengers stepped out.

Just then sirens wailed and the dome lights of three police cars flicked red as they raced to the scene. The Hollisters wriggled to the front of the bus, then jumped down the high step onto the side of the road.

"Oh dear, how did it happen?" Pam asked one of the bystanders. She was told that the load of pigs had shifted on the sharp curve, causing the truck to overturn.

Traffic was halted in both directions, and people began to help the police and the truck driver round up the porkers. Pete and Ricky ran after a small one. They caught it by its hind legs and carried it triumphantly back to the truck driver, who tied up the frightened animal and laid it beside the road.

The pigs were scrambling away.

"Oh, look, Sue," said Holly, pointing up into the woods. "There's a tiny one. Let's get it!"

While the other Hollisters watched policemen and bystanders push the small truck onto its wheels again, the two girls set off after the pig.

"Oink . . . squee!"

When the piglet saw them, it dug its little hoofs into the ground and disappeared behind the trees. Holly dashed for it, tripped and fell flat on her face. Sue continued on, her fists pumping at her side and legs flying.

Suddenly Holly heard Pam call out, "Come on, we're leaving!"

The pig-tailed girl glanced around for her little sister and a frightened look came to her face. "Sue, hurry. We're going back!"

Silence. "Sue, where are you?"

CHAPTER 5

A New Friend

"She was just here," Holly told Pam, who had raced up the slope toward her.

"Did she run into the woods?"

"I suppose so. We were chasing a little pig, and I fell, and—"

Pam did not wait to hear more. She disappeared behind the trees, calling Sue's name loudly. Holly ran back to the bus. The driver, meanwhile, was annoyed by the absence of the Hollisters and honked his horn impatiently.

"Oh dear," thought Pam, "we're ruining everything." She cupped her hands. "Sue, where are you? Sue!"

A big boulder loomed up ahead. Pam ran around it and nearly fell over her little sister. Sue was sitting on the ground, cuddling a small pig in her arms.

"Sue, why didn't you—"

"Shh. Don't wake Piggy. He's tired."

45

Pam took Sue by the hand and pulled her to her feet. "Hurry. The bus is leaving!"

Carrying the squeaking pig under one arm, Sue trotted back with Pam to the road, where the truck driver was loading the last of the pigs.

"My sister caught one for you," Pam said.

The man turned around, surprised. "That doesn't belong to me. That porker's too small!"

"But it fell out of your truck," Pam persisted.

"Well, it must have gotten in by mistake."

"Then can I have it?" Sue spoke up quickly.

"Sure, why not."

"Oh, I have a little pig, really truly all my own!" she declared and patted the small snout in the crook of her arm.

"But—but—Sue—"

The child was much too joyful to notice Pam's objection. While the troopers held up traffic, she scooted across the street and scrambled up the steep step of the bus.

The driver looked at her in disbelief. "What've you got there?"

"A piggy."

"You can't bring him on this bus!" the driver protested.

Sue's face changed from happiness to pain in less time than it takes to twist a pig's tail.

"A—aw!" she cried out. "I want my piggy!"

An elderly lady sitting up front told the driver he was mean.

"But lady, it's regulations!" He explained that the bus could carry small dogs if they were in a satchel. "There's nothing in the rules about pigs."

When one of the troopers heard Sue bawling like a calf, he came over to inquire.

"Wait a minute," he said when he heard of her plight. "I have a carton in the back of my car." He brought the box and Ricky said, "Yikes, that'll make a good pig's house!"

The driver shook his head. In a tired voice he finally said, "All right, get the pig in his house and let's get on with this trip. We're twenty minutes late already!"

In the hours before supper, Sue played with her new pet, and Pam kept Holly and Ricky busy by studying the Braille alphabet. Pete read a magazine. When it became dark, the tired travelers fell asleep one by one. They awakened when the bus stopped late at night.

"Froston! Here's where the Hollisters and their pig get out!" the driver announced good-naturedly.

On the platform stood a lean, rugged man in his sixties.

"Gramp!"

The children yelled in delight as they crowded around their grandfather, exchanging bear hugs with him. Then Gramp glanced at his watch. "You're late. What happened?"

"Oh, it was Sue's pig," Holly explained.

"What? She brought a pig along?"

"Here it is." Ricky picked up the box he had put down on the platform.

"But why—" Gramp's eyebrows shot up.

"It's a long story, we'd better tell you in the car," Pete suggested.

"Good idea. Let's go."

"Where's Gram?" Pam wanted to know.

"Home with our surprise guest."

"And who's that?" Ricky asked.

"You'll find out tomorrow," his grandfather replied as he led the way out of the bus station. Ricky lugged the box with the pig, because Sue was so tired that her legs wobbled.

When they were settled in the car, Pete quickly explained about the pig, then he asked eagerly, "Now tell us about the midnight trolls, Gramp!"

Mr. Hollister grinned as he guided the car onto a highway. "I was waiting for you to ask that question."

Ricky yawned. "There are no such things as trolls. They're only imaginary, aren't they, Gramp?"

"Right. But all the same there are some very odd things going on at Snowflake Camp."

"Like what?" Holly twirled one of her pigtails excitedly.

48

"I don't think we'd better go into it tonight," Mr. Hollister answered. "We'll talk about it tomorrow when you meet our friend."

The car was now far out in the country. As it wound along the road, the cones of light from the head lamps stabbed into the woods.

Sue had long ago fallen asleep on Pam's lap. The others were dozing. Suddenly Holly awoke with a start.

"I see a troll!" she cried.

Gramp put his foot on the brake. "Where?"

"Back there behind those bushes!"

The others were wide awake now as the car backed up and the lights shone on the spot Holly indicated. Nothing stirred in the dark woods.

"Are you sure you saw one?" Pam asked.

"She must have been dreaming!" Ricky spoke up.

Gramp frowned. "What did the troll look like, Holly?"

"All I know is that he was very little."

"Well, whatever it was, it's gone," Gramp said and drove on. A few minutes later he stopped the car in front of a big log house. Around it were several smaller cottages.

"We've enlarged the main cabin since you were here the last time," Gramp explained. "Now you can all stay with us."

The door opened and a round-faced, smiling woman hurried out with open arms.

49

"*I see a troll!*" Holly cried.

"Gram!" the children cried and hugged her. Then she took Sue from her husband's arms, and carried her inside. The others followed.

"Gram," Sue muttered sleepily. "Where's my piggy?"

"We'll put his box in the kitchen beside the stove," her grandfather said and told Mrs. Hollister quickly about Sue's pet.

Then the children were shown to their bunks. Their heads had hardly touched the pillows when they were sound asleep.

In spite of their long journey, they awakened when the first rays of sunlight were streaming through the curtains. Quickly they dressed and hurried into the kitchen. Gram was already preparing hot cereal and scrambled eggs.

Sue trotted over to the stove to see her pig. She did not even notice a little girl sitting at the table. The child was somewhat older than Pam, but smaller. She had dark hair that hung to her shoulders. Her head was bent slightly forward and she looked straight ahead.

"Well," Gram said, laying aside her spatula, "how are my hungry Indians?" Then she added, "Children, I'd like you to meet our guest, Helga Karlsdottir from Iceland."

The children looked at Helga in surprise.

"Hello," she said. "I'm glad to meet you. Your

51

grandmother has told me lots of things about the Hollisters."

By now Pam knew why Gram had called Helga special. The child was blind.

Pam stepped forward and held out her hand. Sensing this, Helga offered hers too.

"I'm so glad to meet you," said Pam. Then she looked at her grandmother questioningly.

"Oh, I know what's on your mind," Gram said. "Why is Helga visiting us here in Froston?"

The children nodded, and Gram went on. "She is the niece of Mr. and Mrs. Peterson, who live down the road from us."

The Petersons, it seemed, had been called away to the West Coast on a family emergency and Gram had offered to care for the girl until they returned.

"I like to come to Canada on vacation," Helga said.

"You speak good English," Ricky blurted out.

The visitor smiled. "My mother is a Canadian. Besides, many Icelandic children learn to speak English."

Holly turned to her grandmother. "We got your letter in code and we figured it out too. There's a blind man who lives near us."

"Yes," Pam added. "Mr. Kovac has been teaching us the Braille alphabet."

Helga's face brightened. "Have you learned it, Pam?"

"Pretty well," Pam replied.

"Good. I brought my Braille playing cards. Perhaps we can have a game later." They were regular playing cards with Braille characters embossed on them.

"That'd be fun," Pam said.

During breakfast, Helga told them that she came from Reykjavik, the capital of Iceland, and that her mother and Mrs. Peterson were sisters.

Holly spread a piece of toast with a thick layer of Gram's homemade jam and said, "Helga, how's your radar?"

The girl thought for a moment and then laughed. "How did you know about that?"

"Mr. Kovac told us."

By this time Pete could wait no longer. "Gram," he burst out, "will you tell us about the midnight trolls?"

"Well, very odd things have been happening here the last few days," Gram began. "Sometimes at midnight we hear an eerie tune being whistled in the woods nearby. Other times it comes from the road—"

"Did you hear anything last night?" Pam asked.

"Yes."

"What does it sound like?" Ricky wanted to know.

53

"It's part of an Icelandic folk song," Helga said. "And last week we found small footprints outside my uncle's house."

"You're kidding!" Ricky said.

"No, she's not," Holly spoke up. "I told you I saw a troll last night!"

"Listen to this," Helga went on. "One time I was sitting under a tree and heard something rustling in the branches. Then came a whispering and chuckling, and then"—she leaned forward and her face glowed with excitement—"an apple hit me right on the head!"

"What's so unusual about that?" Pete asked.

"It was a pine tree!"

The children laughed but Helga did not think it was funny.

"I believe the trolls followed me here all the way from Iceland!" she stated.

"You have trolls in Iceland?" Pam asked.

"Yes. And they disappear just like the hidden people."

"Hidden people? Who are they?"

"Little folks that live in the green hills."

The Hollisters did not want to hurt Helga's feelings even though they believed this was nothing but superstition.

"Let's go and look around for clues," Pete suggested.

The children spent all day searching carefully

around Snowflake Camp and the Peterson house, but found nothing whatsoever.

That evening the weather turned brisk and Gramp asked the boys to build a fire in the fireplace. When it was crackling merrily, Pam begged Helga to tell them more stories about the trolls in Iceland. "And let's just have candlelight," she suggested, "that'll make it spookier. May we, Gram?"

Smilingly Mrs. Hollister lit two candles and put them on the table.

"Would you like to hear about the Yule Cat?" Helga asked.

"Yes. Please. Who's that?" Holly wanted to know.

"A monster who eats all those who don't get new clothes for Christmas. That is why almost everyone, no matter how poor, receives something to wear."

Holly shivered. "I'd rather have Christmas back home. There you get toys."

"Are the trolls mean like this too?" Ricky asked.

"No. They're just a nuisance. You see, there was a lady troll named Gryla. She had a whole gang of trolls under her command.

"One is called Door-Banger. He pesters people by slamming doors."

Just then a strong gust of wind blew across the clearing and the back door of the house went *Wham!*

"Yikes!" Ricky exclaimed. "That scared me!"

Helga went on, telling about another troll named Meat-Hook. "At Christmas time he reaches down the chimney and steals the cookies." Helga glanced about at the Hollisters, for she could realize the looks that must be in their faces. Suddenly a puff of wind came down the chimney.

"Oh—oh—oh!" Holly said in a quavering voice. "Here comes Meat-Hook! Gram, hide your cookies!"

Helga had felt the breeze and gave a little chuckle. "And then there's a bad troll called Candle-Pitcher. He steals children's candles, and of course in the olden days they were very important!"

Just then another puff came down the chimney, and one of the candles blew out.

Suddenly the little pig squealed in the kitchen and broke the spell. All the Hollisters started to laugh.

"I guess we just don't believe in trolls," said Pam, smiling.

"But I saw one," said Holly frowning. "At least, I think I did."

"Tell you what, Holly," Pete said. "Just to make sure, Ricky and I'll go back to that spot tomorrow and look around."

"Now don't you two wander too far from the road and get lost," Gramp said.

"Don't worry. We know the area from our last trip," Pete assured him.

Next morning Sue was playing with the pig, while Pam and Helga helped Gram Hollister bake apple pie. Holly watched fascinated as the thin layers of dough spread out beneath the rolling pin.

Pete and Ricky, meanwhile, hiked down the road to where Holly thought she had seen the midnight troll. With Pete leading the way, the boys pushed through the underbrush, keeping a sharp lookout for anything resembling a troll.

"I think Holly was dreaming after all," Pete said after an hour of futile search. "She was awfully sleepy."

Ricky nodded. "Let's go back."

They had walked only a few steps when the red-head suddenly pointed to the ground. "Look what the troll dropped!"

He picked up a little plaid cap.

Just then someone chuckled. Startled, Pete and Ricky glanced about. The next instant strange wild laughter was coming from the bushes!

CHAPTER 6

Pamela Johnsdottir

RICKY rolled his eyes to look at Pete, and his knees began to shake. "Wha—what is it?"

"I'll find out," Pete whispered.

Again the laughter came. This time Pete advanced through the bushes, but Ricky wanted no part of the search. Instead he turned and ran.

Presently he came to a split rail fence at the edge of a field where horses and ponies were grazing. With a mighty spring he hurtled the fence but his right toe hit the top rail. Ricky cartwheeled in the air and landed with a thud in the green grass.

After lying stunned for a second, the boy let out a keening wail. It carried all the way to his brother who was peering into the bushes. Pete turned and raced after the redhead. He took the fence in one bound, then helped Ricky to get up.

"Did you find the ghost?" asked Ricky, feeling first one leg, then the other, to make sure he had not broken anything.

"No. But I might have if you hadn't yelled as if you were being murdered."

"If that wasn't a ghost," Ricky continued, "it must have been another troll named Bush-Laugher."

"Okay, so it was Bush-Laugher," Pete said. "Let's go back."

The brothers retraced their steps but by now the laughter had ceased and in spite of their search they found nothing.

They set off at a trot and arrived at their grandparents' home to smell the delicious aroma of baking pies drifting from the kitchen.

"They'll be ready soon," said Gram Hollister. Then she looked perplexed at her grandson. "What happened to your back? It's all green!"

"He was running away from a troll named Bush-Laugher," Pete said with a wink, "and did a flip-flop into a pasture."

"There were horses and ponies there," Ricky added. "Good thing I didn't fall on one of them."

"Did you catch the troll?" asked Gramp.

"No," Pete said, "but we have his hat."

"Let's see it!"

Ricky felt in his pockets. They were empty!

"Yikes, I must have dropped it when I ran," he said. "But we can easily find it again, Gramp."

"All right. But I think I'll go with you this time. There just might be something in this business about the trolls."

"Your back's all green!" Gram said.

The trio hastened back along the road, stepped into the woods and searched the area where the boys had heard the laughter. But they did not find the hat!

With Ricky trotting on ahead, they went to the meadow. Still no sign of the hat.

"Maybe one of the horses ate it," said Ricky.

Pete doubted that. "I think the owner returned for it," he said.

Gramp frowned and shook his head. "Are you sure you two rascals aren't putting me on?"

"Honest, Gramp," Pete said. "Everything we've told you is true."

On the way back to his house, Gramp said he would notify the local police just in case anybody was prowling around the cottages.

After lunch the rural postman passed by. He called out from his car that he had left mail at the Petersons.

"Perhaps there's something for me," Helga said. She, Pam, Holly and Sue started for her uncle's white cottage.

The blind girl walked along as if she could see everything clearly before her. When Pam mentioned it, Helga said, "Of course I can see it—in my mind." She went directly to the mailbox and pulled out several envelopes. Then she laughed. "Now you must tell me, Pam. Is there a letter for me?"

"Yes, here's one!"

Helga opened the large flat envelope and pulled from it several pages in Braille writing. She nipped her lower lip in anticipation, and her fingers glided over the raised letters.

"What does it say?" asked Sue, jumping up and down impatiently.

The Icelandic girl gasped in surprise. "Listen to this! Daddy has sent a man named Mr. Hollister in Shoreham a model of his glider invention!"

"That's our father!" cried Holly.

"I can't believe it," Pam said. "To think that our fathers know each other."

They walked back toward Gramp's house. In her excitement Helga had not even finished her letter.

"Now wait a minute," said Pam suddenly, looking puzzled. "Daddy has been writing to a man in Iceland named Karl Sveinsson, but I never heard of anyone named Karlsdottir."

Helga burst out laughing.

"What's so funny about that?" Holly wanted to know.

"It's because we have a peculiar way of naming people in Iceland." Helga explained that Karl Sveinsson was her father. In Iceland, the children of a man named Karl were called Karlsson or Karlsdottir.

"Then if I lived in Iceland," Pam said, "my name would be Pam Johnsdottir."

"That's right," Helga said.

When they reached Gramp's place, she called to Ricky, "Hi, Ricky Johnsson!"

"What?" The redhead looked blank. Quickly the girls told their brothers about the strange Icelandic names.

Gram and Gramp Hollister were equally surprised to learn that Helga's father and their son John had been writing to each other.

"I wish we could go to Iceland!" Pam sighed.

"Yes," Holly agreed. "We could see polar bears and Eskimos and—"

Helga burst out into giggles again. "There are almost no polar bears in Iceland, and certainly no Eskimos."

"No kidding!" Pete said. "I thought there were a lot of igloos!"

Helga shook her head. "Not a one."

Now the Hollisters were all the more curious about Iceland, and began peppering Helga with questions.

She told them how her country, a large island, lay just below the Arctic Circle. It was settled by Norsemen in the year 874. Today Icelanders still speak the language used by people in northern Europe in the year 1000.

"Yikes!" Ricky said. "People in Iceland must be pretty old."

They all were laughing at Ricky's remark when a man came to the door. He wore the uniform of a police officer and introduced himself as a member of the provincial force.

"I got your message, Mr. Hollister," he said to Gramp. "But to tell you the truth, it doesn't sound too clear."

"You mean the trolls?" Ricky blurted out.

"Well, trolls or whatever they are," Gramp said firmly. "I feel pretty sure that some strangers are prowling around here."

"My brothers heard a troll named Bush-Laugher," Holly said. "Isn't that right, Ricky?"

The policeman pulled out a pencil and pad and began making notes of what the children told him. Finally he got up, scratched his head, put his hat on and thanked them for the information. As he opened the door he beckoned to Mr. Hollister and the two stood outside for a moment. Then the officer left.

"What were you talking about, Gramp?" asked Sue.

"I don't think he takes too much stock in our report," her grandfather replied. He added, however, that the policeman would drive past occasionally to check on the cottages.

Later in the afternoon, while Pam, Pete and Helga were talking about Iceland, Ricky dropped down on all fours to give Sue a ride on his back.

"Look, Helga!" Ricky called out. "I'm giving Sue a ride. Arf, arf. I'm a big Saint Bernard dog."

"You're not." Sue giggled. "You're a horse."

Ricky bucked up and down. Sue tried to hold on to his ears, but she fell off and hit the floor with a thud.

As the youngsters played, Pam asked Helga if she had a seeing-eye dog.

"No," the Icelandic girl replied. "But I do have a seeing-eye pony. His name is Thor."

"A *seeing-eye pony?*" All the children wanted to hear about it.

Helga explained that Iceland had many ponies, and that for years they were the only means of going from one place to another.

"Thor is a wonderful pet," she said. "He'll take me anywhere I ask him to go. I miss him so much. I wish I could have brought him."

"Yikes, that would be great," Ricky agreed. His eyes rolled as if he had a secret idea, and he hurried outside.

"Where are you going?" Holly asked.

"Oh somewhere," Ricky said and ran down the road.

Twenty minutes later the Hollisters heard a sudden commotion. Ricky came charging back on a jet-black pony. A man riding a horse raced after him.

He was yelling, "Stop! You little rustler. Stop!"

CHAPTER 7

Setting a Trap

THE hoofbeats and the shouts frightened Helga. "Pam, what's the matter?" she asked.

"Ricky's riding a pony and a man's chasing him."

The redhead guided the swift little beast around the cottages with the man close behind, calling out for him to stop. Finally they drew even and the man reached over to grab the pony's shaggy mane.

Everyone came out of the house and stared in surprise.

"Gracious!" Gramp Hollister said. "Mr. Beem, why are you chasing my little grandson?"

"Your grandson?" the man replied with a look of surprise. "He's a rustler, that's what he is! He stole one of my ponies!"

Ricky slid from the animal's bare back and ran to his grandfather. His face was flushed and frightened. The freckles stood out like big dots on his nose. "I—I didn't steal it," he said, his voice quavering. "I only borrowed it."

"But why?" Gramp asked.

66

"I wanted it for Helga. She misses her seeing-eye pony!"

The man on the horse looked at them, confused. He didn't know what they were talking about.

"Ricky," Gramp said kindly, "you shouldn't take something that doesn't belong to you. That's stealing."

Ricky put his head down and kicked a pebble. Tears ran down his cheeks and into the corners of his mouth.

"I—I didn't steal. I only borrowed the pony."

Seeing that the boy was so frightened, Mr. Beem spoke in a softer voice. "Spook is my best pony. I didn't want to lose him. You can understand, Mr. Hollister."

"Yes," Gramp spoke up quickly. "Ricky was wrong, and I know he won't do it again."

Ricky clenched his fists and hot tears dripped off his chin. "But Helga needs a pony! Can't she borrow it?"

Pam sidled over and put an arm around her brother's shoulder. "I know you meant to do good," she said and looked up to Mr. Beem. "Could we rent the pony for a few days?"

"That's a good idea," Gramp Hollister said. "How about it, neighbor?"

Mr. Beem smiled for the first time. "All right. I'll let you have Spook for a few days. If you need any extra feed for him, you'll find some in the pasture." Then he turned to Ricky and shook his head. "I never saw anybody ride like you, son. Someday you'll be a good cowboy."

Holly spoke up. "But he won't be a rustler any more."

When Mr. Beem rode away, the grandparents returned into the house.

"First trolls, now rustlers," Gramp said. "There's never a dull moment when those kids are around."

Helga, meanwhile, felt for the pony, patted its nose, and ran her fingers through the animal's thick mane. Then, springing light as a feather, she mounted its back, touched its sides with her heels and set off. The others followed.

Helga guided the pony around skillfully. Just as Holly clamored to have a turn, Mr. Beem came trotting back, carrying a saddle and bridle.

Handing it down to the boys, he said, "You'll have a better time with these."

"Thank you," the children chorused and waved to Gramp's neighbor as he rode off again.

Helga slid off the pony and Pete threw the saddle on Spook's back. With nimble fingers, the girl adjusted it, tightened the cinch and arranged the bridle.

"You're real good at it," Pete said admiringly.

"Yikes, for a girl you're great," Ricky agreed.

"What do you mean, for a girl?" Pam protested. "Girls can do things just as well as boys!"

68

"Yes, we could even rustle ponies, if we wanted to," Holly put in and added quickly, "May I have a ride now?"

The youngsters played happily with Spook and when everyone had had lots of turns, Pam said, "I've got an idea."

"What is it?" Ricky asked.

His sister did not reply. She ran into the house and came out pulling her grandmother by the hand. "It's Gram's turn to ride the pony," she announced, laughing.

"Old ladies can't—" Ricky started.

"Shush!" Pam admonished. "Grandma isn't old!"

"She's older than Daddy!"

"Oh, Ricky, this just isn't your day," Pete said and gave his brother a swat.

But Gram Hollister paid no attention. "Wait a minute," she said. "I'll be right out." With that she marched into the house and a few minutes later returned wearing slacks and a blouse.

"Hey, Gram, where'd you get those pants?" asked Holly.

"I bought them to use when Gramp and I go hiking together," came the reply.

With her chin high, Gram walked over to the pony and stepped into the saddle. Then, with a trit-trot, she set off. The children looked on, their mouths agape.

"Look, Gram can really ride!" Holly sang out. She pulled the comeback ball from her pocket and tied one end of the string around her finger. Then she bounced the ball farther and farther away and it sprang back each time.

Now Gram had had enough riding. The pony approached the children just as Holly had given the ball a hard throw. Back it zinged, but the girl failed to catch it. Instead it struck the pony a sharp whack on the flank.

Before Gram had a chance to dismount, the little pet, frightened by the blow, bolted and started to race off.

"Whoa! Stop!" Gram called out, but Spook put his head down, his hoofs flying.

"Runaway! Runaway!" Ricky yelled, bringing Gramp from the house.

"Stop!" Pete shouted.

The pony took one turn around the clearing, with Gram holding onto its neck like an Apache Indian. She fumbled for the reins, but could not reach them.

Pete dashed over to her, trying to head off Spook. As the horse raced past him, the boy flung himself at its neck. His clutching fingers slipped off, but they grasped the bridle. He hung on like a trickriding cowboy, his heels dragging along the ground, until Spook came to a panting stop.

"Hooray! Pete saved Grandma!" shouted Sue.

Gram held on like an Apache Indian.

She ran up, put her hands on her hips, and said, "That was keen. Pete, will you do it again?"

"Not with me in the saddle!" Gram said as she dismounted. "I've had enough!"

All at once the ringing of the telephone came to their ears.

"I'll get it," Pete volunteered. He ran into the house and lifted the receiver. "Oh yes, Mr. Beem. This is Pete Hollister speaking." He listened for a few moments, then said. "Yes, sir. Thanks for telling us."

With that he ran out of the house again, a big grin on his face. Pam was busy tying Spook to a tree. "Who was it?" she asked.

"Mr. Beem. He said there was one thing he forgot to tell us."

"What's that?" Gram wanted to know.

"How Spook got named. He gets spooked and bolts when someone hits him hard on the flank!"

Everyone started to laugh and Holly quickly put the rubber ball back into her pocket.

"How would you all like to hear some stories before suppertime?" Helga asked.

"Will you tell them to us?"

"No, but I have tapes," the girl replied. She explained that recordings were prepared for blind people. "We learn our school lessons that way, and hear all kinds of stories. Come on, I'll show you."

They followed Helga into the living room where

she pulled a portable record player from beside a bookcase. Near it were several boxes of tapes.

The youngsters sat on the floor, while Helga skillfully inserted one of the tapes.

"Oh, goody. It's a Black Beauty story," said Pam, as the narrator began to speak. It kept the youngsters spellbound until suppertime. When the meal was over, Pam suddenly snapped her fingers. "Helga, I have an idea how we can catch those trolls!"

"Really?"

"Suppose we plant the record player in the woods and play the tape, maybe the sound will draw them out into the open and we can capture them!"

"That's a superkeen thought!" Pete agreed enthusiastically. "Why didn't I think of that?"

Gram raised her eyebrows and shook her head slowly. "Now children, don't you think you've had enough excitement?"

"But—"

"Besides, it might not work," Gramp added.

"We could try!" Ricky urged.

"Well," Gramp said, after considering it for a few moments, "you are good detectives, and you just might have a point there."

"Then we can do it?" Ricky asked, dancing up and down."

"Provided *you* behave," Gramp said and gave the redhead a hug.

All the children except Sue set out with the tape recorder. The little girl had been promised a story about the ancient times when Gram was small, so she decided to stay home.

The youngsters advanced a short way into the woods. Helga set the tape to play, then everyone crawled into the thicket and lay waiting to see whether the trolls would show themselves.

It grew darker and Holly began to squirm impatiently. Suddenly there was a noise. *Thump! Thump!* A shadowy figure appeared from the bushes.

Instantly Pete leaped to his feet. "Get him!" he cried.

CHAPTER 8

Tricky Trolls

"WAIT!" Pam called out as the figure became more distinct.

"Yikes!" Ricky cried. "It's Spook. He must have followed us."

"And scared away the trolls too," Pete said, disappointed. "Ricky, Spook was your idea in the first place. Why don't you take him back?"

"Okay!" Ricky jumped up on the pony. "Giddap, boy!"

"And when you come back," Pete cautioned, "don't make any noise!"

Helga rewound the tape on the machine and set it to playing again. The children lay on the ground quietly and listened. Presently there was a slight rustle and Ricky crawled up beside Pete. He whispered, "Gram and Gramp aren't home."

"Sh, sh," Pete warned. "Not so loud."

Ricky lowered his voice to a hoarse squeak. "They're out and I don't know where they went."

"Was Sue there?" asked Pam.

"Nobody. The house is empty!"

"I'm scared," Holly said. "Pam, don't you think we ought to go back? It's starting to drizzle anyway."

Before Pam could reply, a noise was heard in the deep gloom near the recorder. Shivers ran through all of them, and they strained their eyes. But they could not see a thing.

Again they noticed a rustling noise from the bushes ahead.

"Maybe it's a squirrel," Pam whispered to Holly, who was tongue-tied with fright.

Just then there came a muffled sneeze from the record player.

Ricky plucked Pete's sleeve. "Let's go!" he croaked, as the rustling sound moved away from them.

"We'll follow," Pete decided. "Everyone hold hands."

They made an Indian file with Pete in the lead, the smaller children in the middle, and Pam bringing up the rear. But no matter how quickly and quietly they trotted through the gathering gloom, the noise stayed ahead of them.

Suddenly Pete stopped dead in his tracks. The shadowy outline of a small figure appeared ahead. A *troll!*

The boy's heart almost stood still. He turned around and whispered to Ricky.

"Where?" Ricky asked and peered over Pete's shoulder.

"There!"

The spot Pete pointed to was empty. The troll had vanished!

Suddenly there was a loud crack behind them. They whirled around, but nothing moved in the stillness of the forest.

Then Ricky felt a sharp poke in the back. "Ow!" he howled. "Pete, stop that!"

"Shhhh!" Pete said hoarsely. "Stop what?"

"You didn't poke me?"

"Of course not!"

From the bushes came a low chuckling, then crackling noises as if someone was running away.

The children huddled close together, their teeth chattering. For a few minutes they did not dare move. But now all seemed quiet.

"Let's go home," Helga said finally.

"Okay. But we'd better pick up the tape recorder first," Pete said and led the way back to the spot where they had left it.

As they came closer, they heard a wild jabbering.

Helga clutched Pam's hand. "The tape! It's running backwards!"

"The volume's been turned up too!" Pam replied in a thin voice.

Pete gathered all his courage and walked over to

77

the recorder, switched off the machine and picked it up. Then all raced back toward Snowflake Camp.

A pale sickle moon was rising over the treetops as they panted up the road. In front of the cottage they noticed the dim outline of Spook who was tied to a tree. He whinnied softly.

"Gram! Gramp!" Pete shouted. No answer. He opened the door and the children ran inside. The house was empty!

Holly started to cry. "Maybe the trolls took them away!"

"Nonsense," Pam said firmly and put an arm around her sister.

"They can't be very far," Pete said. "The car's here."

He walked outside again and called as loud as he could. Presently a "yoohoo" came from down the road. It was Gram's voice.

"They're at my uncle's house," Helga said. She grabbed Pam's hand and made her way quickly along the path that connected the two houses. The others followed.

Soon a flashlight could be seen crisscrossing the ground in front of the Petersons' place. Gram approached the children, holding Sue in her arms.

"Gram! We've been looking for you. What are you—"

"Somebody has broken in here!" Mrs. Hollister interrupted Pete.

Helga gasped "Oh no!"

"Our lights suddenly went out," Gram went on. "I found only one small candle, but I knew Mrs. Peterson has a whole box of them in her kitchen drawer. I have her key so I walked over here and found that someone must have cut the power line for both houses. The place is a mess!"

"Did you call the police?" Pete asked.

"The phones are dead too!"

"Where's Gramp?"

"Inside. Come on."

They followed Mrs. Hollister into the Petersons' living room, where their grandfather flashed his light around. All was in disarray. Drawers were pulled out from the desk and papers strewn about.

"Your uncle gave us something before he left," Mr. Hollister said thoughtfully. "A box and a large envelope with plans of an invention. Since he was called away on short notice, he couldn't put them in his bank safe and didn't want them unguarded. He said they were not patented yet and were worth a fortune."

"What kind of an invention is it?" Pete asked eagerly.

"An auxiliary motor for a sailplane which he and Helga's father had developed."

Pete snapped his fingers. "Crickets!" he exclaimed. "I'll bet Mr. Peterson is the relative Mr. Sveinsson mentioned in his letter to Daddy!"

The place was a mess.

"I still can't understand how anyone would know about those plans," Gram put in.

"Well, we'll catch those thieves if it's the last thing we do!" Ricky vowed, shaking his fist.

"Let's go outside and look for clues right now," Pete suggested. "May I have your flashlight, Gram?"

"Sure. But hurry up, we'd better go and notify the police soon."

Pete took the light, and he and Pam searched around the house. Soon they found what they suspected. Fresh footprints were visible in the rain-soaked earth behind the house!

One set had been made by heavy boots. The others were smaller.

"You think these were done by a troll?" Pam asked.

"Perhaps," Pete said, "or by small men."

Gramp came to the door and called out, "Pete, you and I will drive to Froston for help."

They hurried to the car, but it would not start.

Gramp set his jaw. "It's been tampered with! Come on. We'll hoof it!"

The road was pitch-black and the beams from Gramp's flashlight bobbed up and down as they walked at a quick pace.

Pete told his grandfather of their experiences in the woods. "I don't believe in trolls," he concluded. "But then, what do you make of this?"

"There could be a connection with the burglary

at the Petersons'," Gramp said. "But on the other hand, this troll business has been going on for quite a while. It's a puzzler all right."

"You know, someone tried to steal the sailplane model Mr. Sveinsson sent to Dad just before we left for Froston," Pete said and explained the episode in Shoreham.

"We'll get the police in on the case. I'm sure they'll be able to clear it up," Gramp replied.

They had trudged about a quarter mile when suddenly they saw car lights far down the road. As the vehicle drew closer, its headlights flashed from bright to normal. Pete and Gramp moved over to the right side.

"Maybe someone in the car is signaling to the thieves!" Pete cried.

As the car sped closer, Gramp grabbed Pete's arm. "We'd better get out of the way!" Together they jumped to the shoulder of the road. But in the darkness they failed to see a deep ditch.

Both tumbled into it, head over heels!

CHAPTER 9

Snaefell Stikki

"Oof!" Gramp Hollister exclaimed as Pete fell on top of him.

"Sorry about that," Pete said and helped Gramp to his feet.

The car, meanwhile, had stopped. "They've discovered us!" Pete whispered.

The two peered cautiously over the top of the ditch. The doors of the automobile opened and a man and woman stepped out. Pete could hardly believe his eyes. "Mother! Dad!" he called and scrambled to the side of the road.

Gramp Hollister followed.

"I thought I saw somebody fall into the ditch," Mrs. Hollister said as she caught Pete in her arms.

"Oh, we jumped," the boy said sheepishly as the four of them stood in the glare of the headlights. "We figured you might be crooks because you were turning your lights off and on."

When Mr. Hollister looked perplexed, Gramp added, "We thought somebody might be signaling to the rascals who ransacked our neighbors' house and then cut off our phone and electricity."

"Gracious!" Mrs. Hollister exclaimed. "Just what has been going on up here?"

"Drive us back to town, Dad," Pete suggested, "and we'll tell you on the way. We'll have to report this to the phone and power companies."

"And the police too," Gramp added.

The car turned around and soon was whizzing back toward the business center of Froston. On the way, Pete said to his parents, "We didn't expect to see you up here!"

"Yes, what brings you to this outpost of civilization, John?" Gramp asked his son.

"Well," Mr. Hollister explained, "I'm really on my way to Iceland. Elaine decided she was going to stay in Froston in the meantime and spend a few days with you and the children."

"Oh, that's great!" Pete put in. "What a surprise!"

"We flew to Froston," Mrs. Hollister said, "and tried to telephone you from the airport, but your line was out of order. So we rented a car and came up."

"But where's your sailplane, Dad?" Pete asked.

"It has been shipped to Iceland by air express. Took three large packing crates to do it," his father replied.

Gramp nudged Pete and said, "Couldn't you tow it up on the back of your jet plane?"

They laughed about Gramp's joke and soon the lights of Froston appeared.

Gramp went into a drugstore that was still open and placed calls to the utility companies and to the chief of the provincial police, who promised to have the burglary investigated. After that they drove back to Snowflake Camp. When they arrived everyone except Gram was asleep.

Mr. and Mrs. Hollister found beds in one of the cottages and drove their car around behind it. Then all of Snowflake Camp was quiet.

Next morning Gram set two extra places at the breakfast table. Holly noticed it immediately. "What's this for, Gram? Are the trolls coming to eat with us?"

Pete, who was pledged to silence, said nothing.

"I know," Ricky said. "It's for the repairmen." He glanced down the road to see two small trucks entering the lane.

Gram just smiled. "You'll see!"

As soon as the electricity was restored, she made a real country breakfast.

When it was ready, everyone sat down.

"Now close your eyes," Gram said, "and don't open them until I tell you!" Through the window she had seen Mr. and Mrs. Hollister walking across the clearing.

When they stepped into the house, Gram put her finger to her lips and motioned to the table. With big grins, the two seated themselves.

"Now open your eyes!" Gram told the children.

Their eyes popped and they stared open-mouthed for an instant. Then four chairs scuffed on the floor as they were pushed back and the Hollisters flung themselves at the visitors.

"Mommy, Daddy!"

"Where did you come from?"

"How did you get here without us knowing?"

"Yikes, and we were expecting trolls!"

After plenty of hugs and kisses all settled down to a jolly breakfast. Introductions were made to Helga and everyone took turns in telling something about the strange mystery that they were trying to solve.

Then, even before the dishes had been cleared, a horn honked outside. Helga recognized it immediately. "Uncle Sig and Aunt Stina!" she said, rising from the table and making her way to the door.

Curious, the Hollisters followed her. A tall man and a small, dainty woman with flaxen hair got out of the car and hastened to greet the girl. Then Helga introduced her aunt and uncle to her new friends. The two men quickly struck up a conversation about Karl Sveinsson's glider propeller, but it ceased abruptly when Gram announced, "I'm sorry to say that your house was burglarized."

"Yikes, and we were expecting trolls!" Ricky said.

Mr. Peterson's expression turned to anger. "I almost expected that!" he said grimly.

Gramp was completely puzzled. "What do you mean?"

"The emergency call to the West Coast turned out to be either a ruse or a mistake," his neighbor explained. "Our relatives knew nothing about it!"

"A lure to get you out of the way!" Gramp exclaimed.

"Right. I'm so glad we had you take care of my papers and Stina's treasures!"

"What treasures?" Holly asked.

Now everyone, including the grown-ups, were curious. They followed Gram into the living room, where she took a brown envelope and a cardboard box out of a wall cabinet and handed them to her neighbors.

Mrs. Peterson took the top off, pulled out a purple velvet jewel case and opened it slowly.

"Ohh!" Pam sighed. In the case were several brooches and other jewelry made from lacy bits of gold and silver.

"What lovely filigree work!" Mrs. Hollister exclaimed.

"My mother has a collection too," Helga said.

Mrs. Peterson told them that filigree was made by Icelandic craftsmen following the tradition of their forefathers. They were experts at bending the silver and gold threads into leaves, roses and other designs.

"Foreign tourists know what they are doing when they buy filigree in Iceland," Mrs. Peterson went on. "Our jewelers do work for kings and queens. Here, look at this!" She showed them a beautiful golden brooch. "This was made for an international exhibition some time ago. There it was stolen, but the thief was caught and the brooch returned. Then I bought it."

Pam looked longingly at a pair of dangling earrings.

"Would you like to try them on?" Helga's aunt offered.

"I'd love to!" Happily the girl fastened the jewelry.

Suddenly Ricky had an idea. "I bet those thieves weren't after Mr. Peterson's invention at all. I think they wanted to get the jewels!"

"It's possible," Pam agreed, as she returned the earrings to the box. "But then why would that man in Shoreham try to steal the plane model?"

"There's no doubt that someone is after those plans," Pete said.

"Well, perhaps there are two separate gangs of thieves," Ricky insisted.

Mrs. Peterson laughed. "Please, don't make it worse than it is." Then she turned to her husband. "Let's go over and see our house."

"It's a mess," said Pam.

It was agreed that all would help to put the things back into place, but first Gram prepared breakfast for her neighbors. The rest of the morning was spent picking up papers, straightening furniture and vacuuming the Petersons' living room. There was nothing missing!

"What I never knew before," Helga's aunt said, "is that there were trolls in Canada. I thought they were only in Iceland."

"But we don't know that there are trolls," Pete said and suggested that they might be local people masquerading in order to escape detection.

Helga moved back with the Petersons, but after lunch walked through the woods to the Hollisters' cottage.

"Uncle Sig wants to go troll hunting this afternoon," she announced.

"That's fine with me," Mr. Hollister said. "We'll all go."

"Don't you think someone should stay and guard the Petersons' house?" Pete suggested.

The grown-ups thought that this would be a good idea. There was still a chance that the burglars might return and ransack the place a second time.

So Mrs. Hollister, Gram and Mrs. Peterson remained at home, while the others set out into the woods. Staying about twenty feet apart, they walked in a line, calling to one another as they went.

The spot where the children had nearly caught the trolls was crisscrossed several times. Pam was amazed to see how Helga avoided the trees using her "radar."

Finally it was Helga herself who made a discovery. Her foot touched something that made a crinkly sound. Bending over, she picked up a piece of paper.

"What's this, Pam?" she asked.

"Looks like a candy wrapper." Pam flattened out the paper and read the name on it. "I've never seen this brand before," she said—"*Snaefell Stikki.*"

Helga gasped. "Uncle Sig! Uncle Sig! We've found a good clue!"

The man came running. "What is it?"

Pam handed him the candy bar wrapper.

"What do you know about that," Mr. Peterson said. "An Iceland candy bar!"

"Then they were really Icelandic trolls!" Ricky said excitedly. "How did they get down here?"

Mr. Peterson replied, "Trolls or no trolls, whoever was here came from Iceland."

"And since they didn't find Uncle Sig's plans, maybe they've returned by this time," Helga said.

"I don't think we have to look around any more," Mr. Peterson said. "This mystery points to one place—Iceland."

When they all hurried home to tell the others, the women were very excited. Mrs. Peterson said, "I've just been told about the Happy Hollisters and the way they solve mysteries. I think they should all go to Iceland, Sig, and get to the bottom of this."

Mrs. Hollister smiled and shook her head sadly. "I don't think that's possible. Frankly, it would cost too much to fly all these children to Iceland."

"Oh, Mom!" Ricky exclaimed, disappointed.

The Petersons looked at each other and smiled. They seemed to have the same thought on their minds.

"I just might have the answer to that problem," Mrs. Peterson spoke up. "Our son Harold runs a charter flying service in Reykjavik. He was due to take some executives to Montreal this week. Perhaps he could fly you back to Iceland."

She went to the telephone. In a few minutes her son was on the line.

"Hello, Harold," she said. "How are you? That's good." Mrs. Peterson listened, then went on, "And Uncle Karl, will he have his sailplane ready?"

Pete hoped the woman would change the subject and talk about flying them to Iceland. He glanced at the others. They all were fidgeting, and Ricky was scratching the freckles on his nose.

After chatting for a few minutes more, Mrs. Peterson said, "Harold, you did fly those men to Montreal?" A pause. "That means you have an empty plane going back to Keflavik?" Pause. "Why do I ask? That's a good question," Helga's aunt said, laughing.

She went on breezily, "Would you have room to fly some friends of mine? Yes, to Reykjavik. How many?"

The woman stopped and mentally counted the children.

"Two adults, Harold, and six children, including your cousin Helga."

CHAPTER 10

The Magic Whale

THE children stood silent and Helga gave Pam's hand a squeeze while waiting for her aunt to finish the phone call.

"All right, Harold," Mrs. Peterson said, "then you will take them along to Iceland? . . . Let me ask them." She turned to the Hollisters. "How about passports?"

"We brought them just in case," Mr. Hollister replied.

"Okay, Harold. Fine. Good-by."

"Yippee!" Ricky cried, doing a handspring onto the sofa.

Pam and Holly hugged Mrs. Peterson while Helga threw her arms around her neck. Pam had never seen Helga so excited.

"You can stay at our home. I'll telephone my mother tonight," the girl said happily.

"But there are seven of us," Pam warned. "Is your house large enough?"

"Oh, sure. We have a guesthouse."

"Boy, now we can see Dad fly his sailplane in the championship meet!" Pete grinned.

Mr. and Mrs. Hollister were speechless. "But this is too much for your son, Mrs. Peterson," Mrs. Hollister said finally.

"Nothing of the kind. He'll meet you at Froston tomorrow morning."

Gramp looked glum. "I thought we were going to have a nice visit here at Snowflake Camp," he said. "And now everybody's leaving us!"

"Don't worry, Gramp," said little Sue and climbed on his lap. "You can have my pig."

Ricky added, "If the trolls aren't in Iceland by now, we'll come back and look for them here."

Preparations went on with whirlwind speed. There were clothes to be washed and ironed, baths to be taken and suitcases to be packed. Helga promised to be at the Hollisters after breakfast the next morning.

When the lights finally went out, it was near midnight. But the excited youngsters were up early next day and soon the Petersons drove over with Helga and her baggage. The girl said she had phoned her parents and they would meet Harold's plane at the airport in Keflavik, which was about thirty-five miles from Reykjavik.

Gram Hollister wiped a tear from her eye as she hugged her grandchildren good-by.

Gramp said, "I'll take good care of your pig,

Sue." He also promised to return Spook to Mr. Beem.

Then the travelers set off in two cars for Froston Airport, where Mr. Hollister turned in his rented automobile. Ten minutes later Harold Peterson landed.

He stepped down, leaving the copilot in the right-hand seat. His parents were delighted to see their son, who looked just like his father.

"So these are the Happy Hollisters!" Harold said, smiling down at the bright upturned faces. "Helga, you certainly do make a lot of friends."

"They're detectives," Helga replied, "and they'll solve the mystery of the midnight trolls!"

Harold chuckled. "Well, good. I haven't seen a troll in years. It seems grown-ups can't find them any more."

Now Mr. and Mrs. Hollister were introduced and the adults chatted for a while. Then Harold winked at his parents and bade them good-by.

"We must hurry," he said. "Luggage ready? Then all aboard!" With a bow and a wave of his hand, he motioned toward the plane. Pete noticed that it was a prop jet and on the nose was painted the name *Snarfaxi*.

Helga told him that *faxi* was the Icelandic word for horse, and a *Snarfaxi* meant a quick-footed horse.

"Like old Spook," Ricky remarked as he climbed up the steps and entered the plane.

Minutes later the travelers fastened their seat belts, the engines whined and soon they were gliding over Froston.

Once high in the sky and heading over the ocean, Harold Peterson left the duties to his copilot and came into the cabin to chat with the Hollisters.

He told them something about the history of

The defenders of Iceland.

Iceland and pointed to the colorful coat of arms on the cabin wall. It was a blue shield and on it were four figures.

Standing on the right side was a giant holding a staff. On the left side was a bull. Over the top of the shield were a dragon and a huge bird.

"Many years ago," Harold explained, "there was a bad Viking king named Gormsson. He wanted to conquer Iceland, so he sent his lieutenant to scout the place. This fellow was magic and turned himself into a whale."

Holly's eyes widened. "A great big whale?"

The pilot nodded. "The whale swam around the island. On the east shore he found a dragon breathing poisonous fire. This dragon was accompanied by giant worms and snakes."

Sue put a hand to her cheek and giggled. "Ugh! That's awful."

"That's what the whale thought too," Harold said. "So he swam away to the north shore."

"What happened there?" Ricky asked eagerly.

"There he was met by a huge bird, like a falcon, whose wings touched the mountains on both sides of a fjord. There were many other birds with him, both big and small."

"So the whale swam away again," Pam said impishly.

"You bet he did. Then he went to the west coast. There he ran into a bull who came charging into the sea, roaring fiercely. With him were the guards of the land, trolls and little hidden people."

"I'd run," Ricky said.

"So did the whale. He swam to the south shore."

"And did the giant chase him then?" asked Holly.

Harold nodded. "This giant's head was higher than the mountain. With him were many other fierce giants. Therefore, the whale swam away and reported to the king that he had better not try to conquer this island."

"To this very day these creatures are known as the defenders of Iceland," Helga added.

"You know any more stories?" Sue asked.

Harold laughed. "I've got to go back. When we pass Greenland, Helga can tell you all about it."

The plane droned on and on. It was a sleepy sound. One after another, the Hollisters dozed off. Several hours later Pete rubbed his eyes and noticed a huge white mountain rising from the ocean over the left wing of the airplane.

"Hey, Helga! Is that mountain over there Greenland?" he asked. Now everyone woke up again.

"The icy one? Yes."

"But I thought Greenland was green," Ricky spoke up.

Helga chuckled. "No, it isn't. Long ago Eric the Red sailed from Iceland to explore a new land to the west. He called it Greenland, saying that men would be eager to go there if it had a good name."

"What a trick!" Ricky said.

"In the summer of 986," Helga continued, "a fleet of twenty-five ships sailed to Greenland. There they settled, and the colony lasted for nearly five hundred years."

"And then?" asked Pete.

"Nobody really knows. But around fifteen hundred the settlement disappeared." Helga told them that hundreds of ruins still stand in Greenland.

Now *Snarfaxi* was leaving the cold, forbidding mountains far behind and before long another vast island loomed up ahead.

"Fasten your seat belts," Harold said through the intercom. "We're about to start our descent to Keflavik."

The Hollisters pressed their noses to the windows hoping to catch a glance of Helga's native land.

Pete was disappointed. "What? This is it? Those barren mountains?"

"Just wait," Helga said.

The plane made a turn on the approach to the airfield. Far below, a harbor could be seen with houses clustering about the shore. Their roofs were red, green, blue—all colors, it seemed to the children.

Finally the plane touched down and hangars rushed past the windows until the craft came to a halt beside a long low building.

The copilot opened the door and let down the steps, pointing out to the Hollisters where they should have their passports checked.

After they had thanked Harold for the ride and bade the two men good-by, they walked down the steps.

A blustery wind swept across the airport and Ricky had to lean into it as he approached the door of the building.

Just then it swung open and a man looked out. Ricky was thunderstruck. The fellow was short and heavy set, with rutted lines in his face.

Instantly the redhead spun around and grabbed his father's arm. "Dad! I just saw the guy who made trouble for Holly and me!"

"Who?"

"The man who tried to steal your glider model in Shoreham!"

"Are you sure, Ricky?"

"You bet. Come on, ask him some questions. Like what he's doing in Iceland!"

The two went quickly inside the building with the others trailing behind. They looked about the waiting room, where customs officials were checking baggage of other travelers. But the fellow was nowhere in sight.

Just then a tall, handsome man came forward and bowed slightly. He said he was from the freight company. "Are you Mr. Hollister from the United States?"

"Yes, I am. John Hollister."

"The one who shipped the sailplane?"

"That's right. Have the crates arrived?"

"Yes, sir. In fact, they got here ahead of time. I wasn't on hand when they were unloaded." The man paused a moment and went on, "I'm afraid I have some bad news for you."

"Bad news?" Mr. Hollister asked with a worried look.

The agent nodded. "The crates have been stolen!"

CHAPTER 11

Teakettle Island

"THAT seems impossible!" Mr. Hollister said. "How could anyone get away with such large crates?"

"It will be hard to hide them," the agent agreed. "That is why I have hopes we will find the thieves soon."

By now the rest of the family and the baggage had arrived in the customs depot. When Pam heard the bad news, she gasped. "Do you suppose those trolls had something to do with it?"

"I think not," Mr. Hollister replied. "If Ricky is right about seeing that man who tried to steal my model back home, I'd say he is the one who is responsible."

The freight agent said the police were already alerted and asked Mr. Hollister where he could get in touch with him. Given the Sveinsson address, he said good-by.

Meanwhile a man, woman and fourteen-year-old

boy had been waving at the travelers from the other side of the customs barrier.

The woman called out, "Helga!"

"Mommy!" The blind girl made her way to the arms of her mother, while Mr. Sveinsson and the boy smiled as the Americans went through customs with their baggage.

Finally Helga said, "Mama, Daddy, Olaf, these are my friends, the Hollisters."

The men shook hands and warm greetings were exchanged.

Pam glanced at the good-looking dark-haired boy who lingered back, a little shy. She whispered to Helga, "Is Olaf your brother?"

"Yes. Olaf, come here," Helga called, reaching out her hand. When he took it, she said, "This is Pam, and over there are Pete, Holly, Sue and Ricky."

"I'm Olaf Karlsson."

Pete liked him. He was half a head taller, had blue eyes, a stubby, turned-up nose and strong chin.

"I didn't know there were five children," he said, speaking English with a slight accent.

"That's what worried me." Mrs. Hollister smiled questioningly at Olaf's mother. "Are you sure you have enough room for all of us?"

Mrs. Sveinsson, who looked much like Mrs. Peterson, laughed. "Of course. Olaf will be the chief of the guesthouse. There's plenty of room for everyone."

"Even me?" asked Sue, turning from side to side on one foot.

"You especially."

The men had been talking together quietly. Mr. Sveinsson turned to his wife. "Anna, something terrible has happened. John Hollister's sailplane has been stolen!"

"Oh no!"

The Icelanders were stunned by the news. "But who would do a thing like that?" Olaf asked.

"It's the trolls," Holly spoke up, "and we're going to catch them!"

"Well," Mr. Sveinsson said, "we can accomplish nothing standing at the airport." He picked up some of the bags. Pete and Olaf helped with the rest. Outside the terminal two cars waited at the curb, a black station wagon and a sporty new Volvo.

"That's mother's," Olaf said with a grin. "I hope she'll give it to me when I'm old enough."

"Neat," Pete agreed.

"Would you like to ride in it?" Mrs. Sveinsson asked.

"Sure."

"Let's have a quick bite to eat before we leave though," Mr. Sveinsson suggested, and they all went to the airport cafeteria.

After lunch Pete got in the front seat of the Volvo. Olaf motioned to Pam and Holly, and the two wriggled in the back together with the Icelandic boy. The remainder of the party climbed into the station wagon.

Suddenly Sue's face puckered up. "I want to go home!" she sniffled as tears streamed down her cheeks.

"Sue, what on earth is the matter with you?" her mother asked. "Why do you want to go home?"

"Cause there aren't any trees up here," the little girl sobbed.

"She's right," Helga said. "Iceland has hardly any trees."

"Then where do the birdies live?" Sue asked.

"They live in bushes or build nests on the ground. We have plenty of birds," Helga assured her.

"You should see the puffins," Mr. Sveinsson added, trying to console the child. "They're very cute."

Sue sniffed and dried her tears, but the look on her face showed she was not really convinced.

Meanwhile the Volvo had started off along a road that skirted the jagged shore line on the left. Off to the right stretched a plain, covered with black chunks of volcanic rock rising to a low mountain ridge. The children bombarded their hosts with questions.

The island, Mrs. Sveinsson told them, was formed by volcanoes, which had erupted from the sea many centuries before.

"It was very hard for the early settlers," she

said. "They had a few cattle and raised some vegetables, but the winters were awfully cold."

"And hardly anyone ever visited them from the other lands," Olaf added.

"Were there trees in Iceland in the olden days?" Pam wanted to know.

"Yes, whole forests," said Olaf. "But they were cut down to build cabins and boats."

"And no one planted new ones," Mrs. Sveinsson explained. "Now the government is growing and protecting trees."

"Like Smokey the Bear," Holly said brightly.

The Icelanders did not know what she meant and Pete had to explain who Smokey was. Then they laughed.

Now the road took a sweeping bend around the rocky coast and on the left they could see a small town.

"That's Hafnarfjordur," Olaf said. "We'll be home shortly."

Holly bent close to Pam's ear and said, "Is Olaf going to be your boy friend?"

Pam blushed, nudged Holly with her elbow and said, "Shush! Of course not."

"Then why do you keep staring at him?" Holly said impishly. For the rest of the way, Pam tried to look only at the scenery.

Finally they passed small houses, and then long

rows of apartments sitting off on the bare landscape past a small green park.

"That's Reykjavik," Olaf said. "We don't live in the city, but in the country on the other side of town."

Holly wriggled around in her seat to wave at the car behind. In the station wagon the two men were talking seriously. Mr. Sveinsson told his visitors about his business. Besides a small pony farm, he had several fishing boats. After the fish were caught, they were dried in the open air on long wooden racks.

"Yikes, how can you eat so much fish?" Ricky asked.

"We don't," Helga chuckled. "It is sent all the way to Africa."

"People there need protein," Mr. Sveinsson said. "Fish is full of it. The Africans boil the dried fish and eat everything, even the juice."

All the way, Sue kept looking around for birds.

"Where are the flying muffins?" she asked, and they all smiled.

"Puffins," said her mother, and after the cars had driven through the town, Mr. Sveinsson pointed into the sky. "There goes a flock of ducks, look!"

This made Sue a little happier, although her mother could tell that she would rather be back in Canada with Gram.

The road now led to broad green pastures and

the Volvo turned into a lane. On the right was a dazzling field of daisies and at the end stood three buildings. The largest was gabled and had a long, sloping roof, painted red and made of corrugated metal. The second house, set a hundred yards away, looked just like it, but was smaller. The third was a barn.

The driveway circled behind the large building and stopped at the small one. As everyone got out, Mrs. Sveinsson said that this was where the children were to stay.

The Hollisters took out their baggage and were shown into the guesthouse.

Pam looked around, delighted. "It's beautiful!" she exclaimed. The walls were of white plaster and on the waxed hardwood floor were bright-colored rugs. A polished wooden staircase was straight ahead.

"I'll show you the bedrooms," Helga said and walked quickly and with great confidence. On either side of the stair was an opening onto a cozy room. Helga and Pam were to share one; the other was Sue's and Holly's. The two younger girls ran in and tumbled onto the soft bed.

Meanwhile, the three boys went upstairs to a large, sunny room with a sloping ceiling. While Olaf helped Pete unpack, Ricky went back to the staircase. He touched the shiny banister with his fingers.

"Pretty smooth!" he thought to himself, "and

just great to ride on." The post at the floor level was smooth too.

Quietly Ricky got on the banister and slid down. "Great!" he murmured. He took the stairs two at a time and straddled the banister again.

"I'll try it no hands this time," he told himself, holding his knees tightly against the smooth wood. But halfway down he started to slip off. His arms flailed wildly and near the bottom his left foot got caught between the balusters.

Ricky let out a howl. "Help! My foot's stuck!"

The girls hastened from their rooms, while the older boys zipped down the stairs.

Holly said, "You silly boy. Look what you did."

"I know it. Ow! Help me get out!"

"Hold still," Pete ordered. Then he and Olaf managed to wriggle Ricky's shoe from his foot. The boy's ankle popped out from between the balusters. He grimaced and limped around a bit, grinning sheepishly. "It was fun anyhow," he said under his breath.

Later, supper was served in the large dining room of the main house. The Hollister children told the Sveinssons about the trolls and that they might have come back to Iceland.

"We don't know if they're involved with the burglary at Uncle Sig's house or not, but we'll find out!" Helga said.

"Help! My foot's stuck!" cried Ricky.

After dinner Mr. Sveinsson telephoned the police, but there was no news about the missing sailplane.

"Time for bed," Mrs. Hollister said finally.

"Yikes, Mother, it's still light!" Ricky protested.

"Look at your watch!"

"What? Nine-thirty?"

Helga explained that this was the land of the midnight sun. "It hardly sets at all during the summer," she said.

"Then how do you sleep?" Holly asked.

"You pull down your shades to keep the light out," Olaf said. "Come on, everyone!"

The children went to the guesthouse. "We'll show you the ponies in the morning," Olaf promised as they parted at the bottom of the stairs. Soon the weary travelers were fast asleep.

Next morning the weather was crisp and cool. The youngsters donned sweaters, and while breakfast was being prepared, Helga and her brother led the way to the barn.

When Olaf opened the door, the Hollisters heard the quiet little noises made by a dozen shaggy ponies in their stalls. Pam sniffed the smell of hay, as she went over to one of the little beasts and stroked his nose. "They look so—so innocent," she said, gazing into the pony's face.

"That's Thor, my favorite," Helga said.

"Your seeing-eye pony?"

She nodded and led her shaggy pet out of the

barn. Helga said a few Icelandic words, and the pony trotted around in circles. At another command, Thor obediently walked back into the barn.

"Later today we'll go on a pony trek," Olaf promised. "But let's have some food first."

When they reached the house, the two men had already finished eating and were on their way out.

"We're going to the glider field near Thing-vellir," Mr. Sveinsson said as the children crowded around the table.

After breakfast, Mrs. Sveinsson packed a picnic lunch for them to take on their trek.

"We'll show you a *hvir*," Helga said. "I'll bet you've never seen one."

"No. What is it?" asked Pam.

"It's a surprise."

"Oh great. And we can look for the trolls too," Ricky said.

They all ran back to the barn, where seven ponies were led out and saddled.

"Sue, can you ride?" asked Helga.

"Course. But I don't see any birds!" Sue replied and glanced about.

"Just be patient."

Pam mounted her pony and whispered to Helga, "Sue hardly ever acts this way. I don't know what's gotten into her!"

With Olaf leading the way, the children followed in Indian file, chatting gaily as the ponies carried them through the green pastures. Now and then shaggy brown sheep glanced up from their grazing, as the troop trotted past. The ground curved gradually upward, and soon the greenness gave way to dark, barren rocks strewn with boulders.

"When are we going to see that funny thing?" Holly wanted to know as the travelers wound higher up the slope.

"It's on the other side of that big rock over there." Olaf pointed.

Pam noticed wisps of smoke rising from behind the boulder. "Is a *hvir* some kind of bonfire?" she asked.

Helga chuckled. "No."

Olaf stopped the ponies near the rock and helped Sue to the ground as the others dismounted.

"Is it scary?" asked Holly.

"No, a *hvir* won't hurt you," Olaf replied. "Come on!"

Cautiously the Hollisters followed their friends. Behind the huge block of lava they saw a crack in the ground. From it rose a column of steam, hissing gently.

Sue clapped her hands gleefully. "Goody!" she cried. "This is a teakettle island!"

CHAPTER 12

Shinbone Secrets

"I LOVE teakettles," Sue Hollister chirped and Pam sighed in relief.

"I thought she was going to cry again," she whispered to Helga.

Now the children hunkered down to look more closely at the steam hole. The vapor formed a small pool of hot water which Olaf said they would use for preparing lunch.

Helga opened a saddlebag and carefully pulled out a container of eggs. Her brother placed them gently in the steaming water. When enough time had passed, he took them out with a spoon. The girls, meanwhile, had set out paper plates stacked with bread, butter and slices of meat.

"Who wants a four-minute egg?" Olaf asked.

Everybody did. After they had cooled, the children nipped off the top with a knife and spooned out the delicious yolks.

When lunch was over and the picnic cleaned up, they mounted the ponies again. By this time Sue had grown sleepy, and Pam set her on the front of her own saddle. The extra pony trailed along behind. By the time they came to the next sight the Icelanders had in store for their visitors, the little girl was sound asleep.

Olaf stopped the ponies some distance from a gurgling, churning pit that bubbled up from the ground. The youngsters wrinkled their noses at the smell.

"It's a sulphur pit," Olaf explained. "We have lots of them in Iceland."

"There must be many fires under the ground," Pete spoke up.

"You're right," Helga replied.

"Any other funny things to see?" Ricky wanted to know.

Olaf turned the ponies around and started for home. "Sure," the Icelandic boy said and pointed at a small pile of stones.

"The trolls built it?" Holly asked.

Olaf laughed. "No. Icelandic people make these. It's called a *varda*. The plural is *vordur*. They were built to indicate the trails."

"In the winter, with snow on everything, it is hard for a traveler to find his way without them," Helga added.

"And the vordur have surprises," Olaf went on as the ponies joggled along. "Inside of them the

116

passers-by used to write little notes, sometimes in verse, to be read by people traveling that way later."

"And guess where they hid the messages," Helga chuckled. "Inside of lamb shinbones. That was the custom."

"Can we stop and have a look?" asked Pam.

"Sure, if you want to."

Sue by this time had awakened and the youngsters got down to examine the varda. They picked carefully through the little pyramid of stones, but found no shinbones.

"Hey!" Olaf said suddenly. "Look!" He pointed to the rough terrain. In the distance, a Jeep was bouncing away from them over a rutted trail.

"Who's that?" Pete asked and shielded his eyes from the sun.

"I don't know," Olaf replied. "Nobody lives out this way."

"Pretty mysterious," Ricky stated. "Think we ought to follow him?"

Olaf glanced at his watch. "We have time. Would you like to?"

"I don't think we should," Pam objected. "This little one is getting too tired." She picked up Sue and held her, and the four-year-old clung to her neck.

It was agreed that the three boys and Holly should follow the Jeep, while Pam, Helga and Sue returned home.

The four urged their ponies to trot so as not to lose the trail of the mysterious Jeep. Olaf had picked up the tire tracks, and pursuit was not difficult. The Jeep had wound higher and higher up the mountain side.

Finally Olaf said, "Pete, I don't know if we should follow him all the way. Maybe it's a hunter driving into the interior of Iceland."

"Let's go just a little bit farther," Pete insisted.

Soon they came to the top of a small rise. Pete and Olaf spied the Jeep. It was parked behind a small hut.

"That's strange," Olaf said. "I wonder what that guy is doing out here."

"Let's go up and ask him," Ricky suggested.

"Not on your life," said Pete. "That's not the way detectives do things." He suggested they take their ponies back down the slope and then creep up and spy on the man first.

The children quickly rode down and tied up their horses on a boulder. Then they crept up on their hands and knees and peered over the rise of black ground.

Suddenly two men came out of the hut. One of them walked around the back, looked at a pile of black rocks, then motioned the other to join him in the Jeep.

"Crickets!" Ricky blurted. "They're coming this way!"

"Run for cover!" Olaf commanded, and the youngsters scrambled down the slope, hiding behind chunks of lava.

They heard the motor of the Jeep roar, but then the sound decreased and soon all was still.

"They left in the other direction," Olaf said and sighed in relief. "Let's go back!"

"What if somebody else is still there?" Holly asked.

"We'll sneak up carefully."

The children quietly approached the hut. It was empty. Pete walked around the back, stared at the pile of rocks for a few seconds, then let out a low whistle. "Olaf! Look at this!"

"That's awfully big for a varda." The Icelandic boy shook his head.

Pete began to pull away some of the stones. Suddenly a piece of wood showed underneath.

"Come on, kids, help us uncover this box!" Pete cried in excitement.

Four pairs of hands threw away the loose stones.

"Dad's stolen crates!" Pete exclaimed. "One— two—three of them!"

"We've found his sailplane!" Ricky cried out.

A quick search over the boxes showed their father's name and the destination to which the sailplane had been shipped. One of the crates was open.

"Dad's stolen sailplane crates!" Pete exclaimed.

"That was a clever hide-out," Olaf said, utterly amazed.

"Hurry. We must get back and tell Daddy," Holly declared.

Without waiting to search the old hut, the youngsters raced back to their ponies, mounted up and galloped toward the Sveinsson farm.

Flushed with excitement, they reached the barn in a short time. The men had just arrived from Thingvellir and were stepping from the car.

The young detectives rushed up to them. "Dad! We've found your sailplane!" Pete said breathlessly.

"What?"

"And we've got to get it right away before those bad men come back!" Holly urged.

"You really found it?" Mr. Hollister asked and could hardly believe what he heard.

"Sure," said Ricky. "We trailed the bad guys."

Speaking rapidly in Icelandic, Olaf told his father about the day's event.

"All right," said Mr. Sveinsson, ready for action. "I'll get my truck, John." He hastened to the garage, built on one side of the stable.

Presently he backed out a sturdy-looking pickup truck. The two men hopped in.

"Room for two more," Mr. Hollister called out and beckoned to Pete and Olaf.

"We'll tell the others meanwhile," Ricky said. "Come on, Holly."

They dashed into the house while the four set off at top speed in the direction of the mysterious hut. As they drove along, a long whip antenna beside the truck cab swayed in the wind.

Mr. Sveinsson plucked a microphone from the dashboard and called the local police on his two-way radio.

Five minutes later a helicopter appeared, circling over the area, and two Jeeps appeared on the scene. All converged on the hut at the same time. The chopper landed and a policeman stepped out. He was joined by other officers spilling from the cars.

They made note of the stolen goods, glanced quickly into the hut, then helped Mr. Hollister and his host to load the crates on the truck. One of the policemen drove his Jeep a distance away and remained as a stake-out. Then everyone left.

That evening all were in a gay mood in the Sveinsson house. The lost had been found, and Mr. Hollister planned to test-fly his sailplane the next day.

"Thanks to my young detectives," he said, smiling at them.

"I hope the police will catch those men soon," Olaf said at the supper table. "We described the two we saw as well as we could."

"And I gave them a description of the man who tried to steal the model from Ricky too," Mr.

Hollister added. "I'd like to see them round up all three."

"I still wonder where the trolls fit in," Pam mused.

"Maybe they've disappeared," Sue said.

"Well, boys, how would you like to go fishing tomorrow?" Mr. Sveinsson suggested. "There's a wonderful salmon stream that runs right through town."

"Crickets!" Pete exclaimed. "That would be great. Do you have some spare tackle, Olaf?"

"You can use mine," Helga said, and Ricky continued to be amazed at how many things a blind girl could do.

"And I know where we'll go," Helga said, turning to the girls. "The museum. We've a wonderful national museum, full of interesting things."

Next morning the men departed with the crates. The girls were driven to the museum, while the boys got fishing rods and set off on ponies to a rushing stream about a mile away.

As the shaggy little ponies pushed along, Pete looked up at a hill south of Reykjavik and said, "Are those big tanks up there for oil storage, Olaf?"

"No. They're water tanks."

"You're kidding."

"No. Really." Olaf told Pete and Ricky that water from underground hot springs was piped into the huge tanks. "It's used to heat all the houses in town," he said.

"Very economical," Pete said. "You get it right from nature."

"We have warm swimming pools too. We'll try them while you're here."

"Oh yes!" Ricky said. "But not until I catch a big salmon!"

The boys reached the small river and dismounted. After tethering the ponies, they took their fishing rods and walked across a rough field to the edge of the stream.

The swirling, rushing water was about thirty feet across and did not appear to be very deep. Olaf attached artificial flies to the lines and the boys cast them into the stream.

"Let's see who catches the first one," Olaf said with a grin. "Usually the visitors do."

Pete and Ricky often had gone trout fishing with their father and knew how to handle a fly rod. After the first cast, they whipped their lines back and forth, looking for a likely eddy where a fish might be waiting.

Nothing happened for a few minutes. Then Olaf's prediction came true. Pete felt a strong tug on his line and knew he had something.

"Wow! It's a whopper!" he cried out. He played the salmon for a few minutes. It turned this way and that, leaping from the water in an effort to get free, but the hook held tight.

Ricky became so excited that he laid his gear aside and scrambled to the bank of the stream. "I'll help you get him out!" he called.

Pete moved back farther. He wanted to land the fish himself, but before he could tell Ricky to stand away, the redhead reached over for the line.

He grabbed it and began to pull the flopping fish toward the shore. He leaned over too far and suddenly lost his balance.

Ricky fell headlong into the swirling stream!

CHAPTER 13

The Skilligan

ALTHOUGH Ricky could swim, he had a terrible time in the foaming, churning water of the salmon stream. As he shouted for help, Pete and Olaf raced along the bank.

Pete kicked off his shoes and started to peel off the light jacket he was wearing. "Keep swimming, Ricky! I'm coming after you!" he shouted.

"Wait a minute, Pete! I have an idea!" Olaf said and, whipping his fishing rod back and forth, sent the baited hook in Ricky's direction. For a second it drifted over the frightened boy. Then, with a quick movement the Icelander set the hook in Ricky's pants. The pole nearly bent double.

Olaf pulled gently so that the fishing line would not snap. Slowly he eased Ricky toward the shore until he could make it up the stony bank. As the redhead dripped toward him, Olaf reeled in the line and Pete quickly removed the hook from his brother's clothes.

126

"Thanks, Olaf," Ricky said. "I thought the salmon would bite me!"

"You're lucky you didn't drift out into the sea where Gormsson's whale might have swallowed you!" Pete grinned.

The three boys considered what to do. Ricky was too embarrassed to return home looking like a wet sponge. But he could not take off all his clothes to dry them there either!

Olaf had an answer to the problem. "Let's go to the warm water pool. We can rent swim trunks, and Ricky's clothes will dry while we're having fun."

Pete tied his salmon to the pommel and the furry ponies carried them to Reykjavik's large outdoor pool.

Inside, the boys rented white trunks and got their lockers. Ricky spread his clothes out to dry in the sun, then the three jumped into the pool. The water was warm and relaxing.

"Yikes!" Ricky called out. "This is like taking a bath!" The trio splashed around, swam underwater, played tag and had a good time for nearly an hour.

"I'm sure your things are dry by now," Olaf said finally. They toweled themselves, dressed, mounted their ponies and joggled back toward the Sveinsson home.

On the way a car passed them and honked.

"The girls!" Pete called out as Mrs. Sveinsson

brought the Volvo to a stop. "How was fishing?" she asked.

"Great!" Pete replied with a wink at Olaf and showed the big salmon he had caught.

"Did you have fun at the museum?" Ricky wanted to know.

"Oh yes," Holly replied, leaning out of the window to pet his pony's nose. "There were old coins and ancient dresses and furniture—"

"But I liked the skilligan best," Sue piped up.

"The what?" Pete asked.

But Sue just giggled and squirmed in her seat as the car started off again, leaving the ponies behind.

Mrs. Sveinsson fixed the salmon for lunch, and the two men arrived from the airfield in time to enjoy the excellent meal.

"John's plane is all put together," Mr. Sveinsson said.

"Thanks to your help," Mr. Hollister added. He turned to the children. "I'm going to test-fly it this afternoon. Who wants to watch?"

"I do! I do!" they shouted.

Mrs. Hollister put her hands over her ears. "Goodness," she said. "They'll hear you all the way to the airport!"

"I can understand their enthusiasm," Mrs. Sveinsson said, leaning over to pat Holly's head. "Let's all go and see the take off."

The ride to the airfield led past a huge pipeline

carrying hot water into the city. It stretched like a fairy-tale dragon alongside the road, which twisted and turned, uphill and down, until it led into a large grassy valley.

In the distance the Hollisters could see a small airplane hangar. Half a dozen sailplanes were parked alongside of it.

As they came closer, they heard the roar of an engine. It sounded as if an airplane were about to fall on them. Pete glanced up to see a one-man helicopter whizzing not more than fifty feet from the ground.

It shot past like a bullet, soared higher, and returned to make another deafening pass over the car. This time the Hollisters had a better look at the strange craft.

It was not enclosed and a man sat in the open air with the control stick between his legs. Overhead was a single rotor and directly behind the seat roared an airplane propeller.

As the Hollisters pulled up to the hangar, the chopper swooped down and alighted beside them.

The pilot cut the engine, jumped out and walked over to Mr. Sveinsson. They spoke in Icelandic for a few moments.

"Dad is telling Mr. Kristinsson who you are," Helga explained to Pam.

Now the man turned and in halting English said he was glad to meet the Americans. He wore a

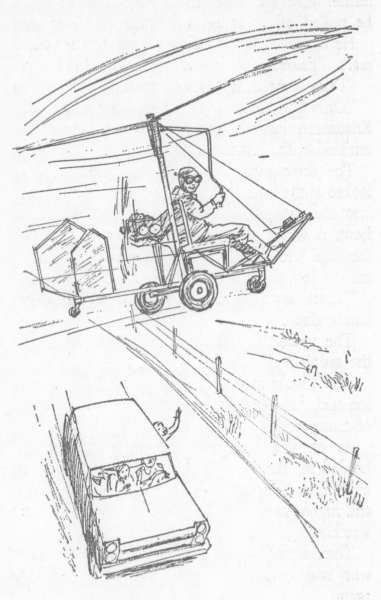

It shot past like a bullet.

leather jacket and a Red Baron flying helmet, which he pulled off to reveal a headful of blond hair.

He motioned to the children to step closer to his craft. "Examine it if you want to," he invited.

"Does it hold only one?" asked Ricky.

"Only one, unless someone sat on my lap." Mr. Kristinsson laughed and the corners of his eyes crinkled with humor.

The three men walked to the sailplane. They looked at the instruments and Mr. Hollister climbed into the cockpit. A towline was attached to the front. A winch some distance away started to pull the rope and the glider skimmed along the green grass a few seconds before zooming skyward.

"There goes Daddy," said Sue, clapping her hands gleefully.

The youngsters watched the towline drop and the sailplane level off.

"He'll make for that hill over there," Mr. Sveinsson said, "and pick up a thermal—that is a current of rising air."

As he had predicted, the glider banked and headed for the barren mountain. It was lifted up, up, up, as if by an invisible hand, circling higher and higher until Pete got a crick in his neck from watching.

Their attention was diverted by Mr. Kristinsson, who said good-by and took off in his helicopter again.

Pete asked Olaf more about the friendly pilot. Mr. Kristinsson, he was told, was a man who printed books and flew his chopper as a hobby.

"He belongs to the Icelandic Air-Sea-Rescue Patrol," Olaf said and added, "He lives on that little farm over there, see?"

The copter, now very high, was heading toward a red and white cottage, which looked like a glob of color far out on the meadow. The chopper soared over the spot, but then, like a stricken bird, it dropped suddenly downward.

"Oh!" Pam cried out. "It's going to crash!"

The others were startled too. The helicopter disappeared behind the cottage in an instant.

"Did you see that, Karl?" Mrs. Sveinsson called anxiously to her husband.

"No. I was watching for John. What was it?"

When told about Kristinsson's sudden disappearance, Mr. Sveinsson was not at all disturbed. "That's all right," he said. "He lands like this all the time. He's the best in Iceland."

Relieved, the youngsters again scanned the sky for Mr. Hollister. Half an hour later he came into view. The sailplane circled lower and lower, then dropped down onto the airfield and skimmed the grass to a halt, not far from the hangar.

The children ran out to greet their father. He opened the hatch and jumped out. "Karl, she's working perfectly!"

"Great!"

On the way home the men quietly discussed possible reasons for the theft of the sailplane.

"I wonder why only one of the cases was open," Mr. Hollister said thoughtfully.

"Well, the thieves wanted to make sure they got the right thing," Mr. Sveinsson said.

"But they picked the one with the fuselage. Maybe they thought—"

"That the invention had already been built and was on it?"

"Exactly."

"It's possible," Mr. Sveinsson agreed. "But we don't know for sure."

For the rest of the day the children played with the ponies. Helga hitched Thor to a cart and they took rides around the field.

Twilight settled ever so slowly over Iceland. By the time the children went to the guesthouse, the sun hung low over the rim of the horizon. Later, clouds moved in and the night grew darker.

Holly had trouble falling asleep. The excitement of the day kept running through her mind. "Sue, are you awake?" she whispered.

"Uhu," came the sleepy reply.

"Let's talk." Holly climbed into her sister's bed.

"Is the sun still out there?" Sue wanted to know.

"Should we go and see?" Holly suggested.

Since their bedroom window faced the east, the

133

two girls padded into the hall and went to the front of the house which looked west.

The horizon was a faint, pale strip of light pasted on the edge of the world. On top of it, like a hat of feathers, sat a puffy jumble of dark clouds.

"The sun's gone to bed too," Holly said with a sigh. As she turned to leave, Sue suddenly grabbed her arm. "Look! I see a skilligan!"

"What?"

"Over there!" Sue pointed to the big house.

"I don't see anything," Holly said.

"It's gone now," Sue added.

Holly looked once again just to make sure. Then, in the dim moonlight, she noticed something that made her gasp.

Two pointed hats rose up slowly from behind a low hedge!

"Trolls!" Holly shouted. She dashed out into the hall.

"Help! Trolls!" Sue echoed shrilly. "Wake up, everybody!"

Upstairs the boys could be heard tumbling out of bed. Seconds later they pounded sleepily down the stairs. At the same time the older girls burst from their room.

Breathlessly Holly told what she had seen.

"Are you sure?" Pam asked quickly and followed the boys to the door.

"Sure I'm sure."

"And I saw a skilligan!" put in Sue excitedly.

In their bare feet Olaf and Pete dashed along the path to the house.

"There is somebody!" exclaimed Pete as he saw a tall dark figure slipping around the corner of the building. Then a second man followed him!

Olaf yelled something in Icelandic. Lights went on in the big house as the prowlers melted away in the darkness.

CHAPTER 14

Pinpoint Messages

Mr. Sveinsson and Mr. Hollister were out of the house in a second, carrying flashlights.

"Holly, take Sue inside," Mr. Hollister called out as they joined in the hunt for the prowlers.

As the two girls disappeared through the door, the searchers spread out, covering a large area. But they could find no one.

"No use chasing them any further," Mr. Sveinsson finally declared. "We'll never catch up with those crooks."

The children followed him into the house, where he quickly alerted the police. He also asked the sergeant on duty if anyone had returned to the mysterious hut.

Nobody had, he was told, but a man was seen spying on the place through binoculars.

"Then the thieves know that we've recovered the sailplane," Pete deduced. "Now they may never go back to their hide-out!"

Pam was still curious about what Sue had called a skilligan.

"It's a thing with stripes," the little girl explained. "Like the one we saw in the museum."

Holly suggested that they return there next day. Perhaps it could turn out to be a good clue.

Mrs. Sveinsson promised to take them, but told the youngsters to go back to bed now. "And make sure to lock the door, just in case," she added.

The following morning the children awakened early. As they ran out into the bright sunlight, the troll scare was forgotten. Helga suggested a game they could play before breakfast.

"There's a varda in the back of our field," she said. "Let's pretend that we are travelers and leave notes for each other."

Olaf went to feed the ponies. Pete joined him and Sue tagged along too. The others formed two teams. Helga and Holly were on one side, Pam and Ricky on the other.

"Do you see the varda?" Helga asked Pam.

The Hollister girl shaded her eyes and scanned the back part of the farm. "Oh yes, it's sticking up over there," she said.

"Right," Helga said. "Do you see it, Holly?"

"Yes." The little girl bobbed her head up and down.

"Then take me to it," Helga said, "and we'll leave a note."

With that, she and Holly set off hand in hand across the field. It seemed like quite a while before they returned, and Ricky was already grumbling about the delay in the game.

"Give them time," Pam said. "There's no hurry."

"I still don't see what takes them so long."

But before Pam had a chance to reply, the two girls came running back. Holly was full of giggles. She had a secret, but wouldn't tell them.

Immediately Pam and Ricky dashed off. The high grass and the daisy stems tickled their knees as they skipped over the sweet-smelling fields.

Finally they reached the varda. Ricky immediately began removing the stones from the top. "Yikes, where is that note?" he asked impatiently.

Pam got down on hands and knees to examine the layer of stones nearest the ground. She cocked her head and saw something white tucked far under.

"Here it is!"

Ricky's hands were smaller than Pam's, so he reached in and pulled out a small bit of cardboard. Quickly he looked at both sides of it.

"There's nothing on it, Pam. It's a fake!"

"Let me see." Pam studied the bit of cardboard more closely and noticed little pinholes in it.

"Ricky, it's in Braille!"

"What does it say?"

Pam spelled out the message. "You and Ricky are very tricky to find the varda note so quickly."

"Yikes, Helga can write verses in Braille!" Ricky said. "She's good!"

The children replaced the stones, then ran back to the house where breakfast was waiting. Taking her seat at the table, Pam said, "Helga, we found your tricky message!" She added, "I didn't leave any, because I had no pin."

"You should always carry one with you," Helga said in mock seriousness as she lifted a spoonful of hot cereal.

When breakfast was over, the youngsters piled into the station wagon like wriggling Icelandic herrings and soon were at the door of the National Museum.

"Now show us the skilligan, Sue," Pam said, taking her sister's hand as she walked up the stone steps.

Sue led the way into a large room lined with cases of ancient relics.

"Here's where the skilligan is," she said.

"Ugh! That's scary," Holly exclaimed.

They stood before the skeleton of an ancient Icelander, curled up in exactly the same way in which he had been found years before. With it were beads and broken parts of old utensils.

"A skeleton!" Pam said. "Is that what you saw prowling around the house, Sue?"

"Here's the skilligan!" Sue said.

Sue nodded.

Pete and Olaf, who had lingered behind, looked at each other questioningly. Perhaps the prowlers were trying to scare someone!

"Surely *we* don't believe in ghosts," Pete said.

"Well, some people do," Olaf remarked. "There are Icelanders, for instance, who have ESP. Don't call it a superstition either!"

"All right," Pete said. "No offense, Olaf."

The museum curator, a short, well-dressed man with gray hair and light blue eyes, was passing by. Seeing the Hollister party gathered around the exhibit, he stopped and asked if they had a special interest in it.

Pam did not tell all of the mystery, but she revealed enough to let him know they were detectives.

"Oh good," he said with a smile. "Perhaps you can help us. All kinds of things were hidden in the olden days. There is one treasure in particular that we are looking for."

"What's that?" Pete asked, edging forward.

"A bag of ancient coins, some of them from the Roman Empire." The curator went on to say that a recently discovered parchment told of the coins being buried by a chieftain in a varda near Reykjavik.

"We're having a search made of all the vordur in the area. Perhaps you would like to help."

"We certainly will," Pam said and added, "They wouldn't be hidden in a shinbone, would they?"

"No. The parchment relates that the coins are in a bag made of silver chain."

"Yikes, let's start right away!" Ricky said, running toward the door. The others followed, waving good-by to the friendly curator.

As they got into the car, Mrs. Hollister said, "Don't you think you'd better tackle only one mystery at a time?"

Pete shook his head and grinned. "The more, the better."

They arrived home shortly before lunch. Mrs. Sveinsson said she had planned a trip to town to a certain silver shop in the afternoon. "They are making a beautiful filigree brooch for me," she explained. The girls clamored to go, but the boys decided to look for the varda treasure instead.

With sandwiches in their saddlebags they set off on their ponies.

The girls had lunch at home, then drove to town. Mrs. Sveinsson parked the station wagon on Adalstraeti and led the way to a small silversmith shop. The proprietor, a stout man with rimless glasses, greeted her cordially in Icelandic. After hearing Mrs. Hollister speak English, he did the same.

"Work is progressing on your pin, Mrs. Sveinsson," the man said. "Take a seat here, and I will show it to you."

The women and Helga sat down on low stools before a glass case while Pam and Sue viewed over their shoulders at the half-finished brooch, which the silversmith set upon a piece of black velvet.

"It is charming," Mrs. Hollister said.

While they chatted with the silversmith, Holly glanced around the shop.

To the rear, a small door led down two steps to a tiny workshop. She peered inside to see two men sitting before a bench. One was regular size, the other was a midget.

Just then the sound of music drifted into the shop. Holly turned and skipped to the door. Down the street came a brass band, led by a jaunty drum major. Behind him marched men in red and blue uniforms, blowing on their horns as they kept briskly in step.

BOOM! BOOM! sounded the big bass drum!

Holly loved to hear a band. Sue and Pam did too, and hurried out to the sidewalk. After the parade passed by, a throng of children followed.

Holly joined them as they turned a corner and entered the square before the Iceland Parliament building. There the march ceased and the players mounted the bandstand. Holly was so excited that she pulled the comeback ball from her pocket and began to bounce it. Suddenly the rubber string broke and the ball rolled under the bandstand.

"Oh dear," Holly thought. "Now what?" Maybe Pam could help her. She looked around for her sister, but could not see her in the crowd.

"Well, I'll have to get it myself," Holly decided and wriggled under the platform. Quickly she grabbed the ball and was about to retreat when she saw two big feet blocking the way. She poked her head out from under the bunting and looked up into the face of a policeman!

CHAPTER 15

The Ski Lodge Ghost

WHILE Holly was staring up at the policeman, her brothers and Olaf were on their way in search of the ancient vordur.

"We'll have to look for a real old one," Olaf said.

"How can you tell?" Ricky wanted to know.

Olaf explained that they would travel on unused trails, the nearly forgotten paths of his ancestors.

"The vordur will probably be weathered and the stones scattered about," he said.

An old trail led the boys part way up the base of a mountain. White snow still lay in some of the crevices.

"We have great skiing here in the winter," Olaf remarked.

Pete and Ricky took in the distant view. They were now one quarter way up, still on a gentle slope. Behind them, wild and desolate countryside stretched far away to the sea.

Pete was examining a varda. He dug away the

gray stones, but found nothing. Olaf and Ricky had had no luck either, yet.

About noontime they found a place to sit down with their backs against the boulders and ate their sandwiches.

Ricky stretched. "It'll take us a couple of years to check out all the vordur on Iceland," he said with a note of disappointment in his voice.

"Cheer up," Olaf said. "Maybe we'll find some *huldefolk* to help us."

Ricky remembered Helga's telling about the little creatures.

"What do they look like?" he asked.

"The hidden people wear clothes of many colors," Olaf replied, "and have pale, gentle faces."

The redhead glanced about anxiously. All was silent. Nothing moved between the lava chunks, which were of all sizes and queer shapes. One could imagine they were all sorts of things. Some of the boulders seemed balanced as if ready to roll off any moment.

"Funny thing about those trolls," Olaf continued and munched the last bite of his sandwich. "They don't go about in daylight."

"Why not?" Pete asked.

"They would turn to stone." Olaf told of an old woman troll who was hurrying home carrying a big fish on her back. "It was nearly daylight. She had to go fast or else—"

"Did she make it?" Ricky asked anxiously.

"No," Olaf replied, wiping a crumb from his chin. "Daylight came before she got there and she was changed to stone.

"To this day," he concluded, "the old lady stone troll with the fish on her back can be seen by visitors on the northwest coast."

Ricky shivered a little. "Don't tell us any more spooky stuff."

Pete gave Olaf a wink. "What do you make of the skeleton Sue claims she saw?"

"Well, I don't know. About fifty years ago a skier disappeared in a crevice up there." He pointed, and his companions looked up the mountainside.

"There's a ski lodge around that ridge," Olaf went on, "and people say his ghost comes back and his bones rattle in the lodge. Maybe he took a walk and came to our house—"

Ricky gulped and Pete slapped him on the shoulder.

"What's the matter, Rick? You don't really believe these stories, do you?"

Ricky managed a half smile. "Course not." He rose to his feet and looked all around suspiciously.

"I'd like to see the lodge," Pete went on. "Is it far from here?"

"Not too far. But it's closed now. And part of the way we'll have to climb on foot."

"Okay. Maybe we can find the treasure varda on the way. Are you coming, Ricky?"

"Sure!"

The ponies carried the boys several hundred feet farther up the mountainside, until the way became too steep for the animals.

"Here's where we tether our ponies," Olaf said. He got off and tied the beasts to a small jagged rock. They stood quietly. One pony, who had a smiling expression, turned his head to watch the three companions as they began to climb up the stony hillside.

The trail was faintly marked, because, Olaf said, hardly anyone ever ventured up there during the summer.

After a few minutes Ricky stopped to catch his breath. "Do you suppose we can hear the ghost's bones rattle?" he asked.

"Never can tell," Olaf said.

The hikers had to bend over to keep their balance, and sometimes the loose stones clinked and clanked down the trail behind them.

Pete stood up straight to rest for a moment. His eyes wandered to the ridge above. There he saw a dark figure looking down at them!

He grasped Olaf's arm and pointed. The Icelandic boy only laughed. "That's only a weird rock formation."

Pete pointed to a figure on the ridge.

"How much farther is the ski lodge?" Ricky asked.

"Just around this gully," Olaf told him. "There's one edge of the roof already."

"Oh good." The redhead set off briskly again, but suddenly he, too, noticed something. This time it was a glint coming from behind a boulder not more than a hundred yards away. "There's a troll!" Ricky cried. "It jumped behind that rock over there!"

When the older boys questioned him, he admitted, however, that it was only a flash he had seen.

"It could be someone spying on us with binoculars," Pete declared.

Olaf nodded. "Let's go and find out."

All three started in the direction of the boulder.

"What do you make of it?" Pete asked his friend. "Why would anybody be spying on us?"

"To scare us away perhaps!"

"But why?"

Olaf did not answer. He was staring at the ground, where a small slip of orange-colored paper lay half hidden under some pebbles.

The Icelander bent down and picked it up. The paper was dry and unwrinkled, indicating that it had been dropped there only recently.

"What is it?" Pete whispered.

"A bus ticket. Keflavik to Reykjavik."

Ricky, who had hurried on ahead, heard Pete's low whistle, turned, and was beckoned back.

"Look, we'll have to be very careful," Olaf said. "I'm convinced somebody really *is* up here."

"Maybe looking for the ancient varda," said Ricky.

"Right. So let's not take any chances."

Walking carefully, in order not to disturb the loose stones, the three boys crept up on the boulder. They reached it, but hardly dared to look around the other side. They waited for a moment, listening, then they heard a noise!

Tap—tap—tap.

A chill of fright wriggled through Ricky. His eyebrows lifted toward his red tousled hair. He grasped wildly at Pete.

Tap—tap—tap came the sound again.

"It's the gh-ghost of the sk-ski lodge," Ricky quavered. "He's rattling his bones!"

"Wait a minute! Don't get—!"

But Ricky turned and started down the hill as fast as he could go, skidding and sliding in a frantic effort to reach the ponies! Faster and faster he went, unable to stop!

"Let's get him before he hurts himself," Pete cried.

Olaf glanced at the boulder. Like Pete, he wanted to investigate further. But now Ricky was in danger!

Together they hastened down the hill, at the same time calling to the frightened boy.

"Take it easy, Rick!" Pete yelled. "We're coming!"

As they caught up with him, they rounded a screen of rocks and boulders. Right below them was the place where they had tethered the ponies. All three stopped short and stared in disbelief.

The animals were gone!

CHAPTER 16

The Copter Captive

"Somebody's stolen our ponies!" Pete cried out.

"Yikes," Ricky said. "Now we're stranded!"

Olaf tried to keep his cool. "Let's see what we'll do now."

They talked over the situation quietly. Someone had apparently been spying on them. The person behind the boulder must have had an accomplice at the foot of the mountain, watching for anyone who might come along.

"But why would they do that?" Ricky asked.

"Because they have something to conceal," Olaf reasoned. The boys made several guesses as to what it could be. Stolen loot, perhaps? Or a hide-out?

Pete thought that the flash which Ricky had seen could have been a mirror signal to the person at the base of the hill.

"I think the ponies were taken to discourage us from coming back here," Pete said.

Olaf glanced at his watch and frowned. "It

would take a long time to reach home, even if we ran all the way."

"Nothing to do but hike," Pete said. "Let's go, gang."

They decided to walk briskly but not to run in order to preserve their energy. As they scanned the distant ridge, they noticed a small black dot in the sky which slowly became larger. Then the telltale noise of an engine broke the silence.

"It's the helicopter man!" Ricky cried out.

The three boys jumped up and down and waved, hoping to attract Mr. Kristinsson's attention. The craft nosed down, slicing parallel to the slope like a roller coaster. It hovered for a few seconds, then settled to earth near the hikers.

The pilot stepped out, pushed back his goggles and unstrapped his flying helmet. "What are you doing out here?" he asked.

"Some thieves stole our ponies, and we have to walk home," Olaf replied.

Mr. Kristinsson scratched his head. "Aha, so that was it. I saw a man on horseback, leading three ponies, and wondered what he was doing with all these animals."

"Would you catch him for us?" asked Pete.

"I might. But who would return the ponies?"

Ricky, who felt a little ashamed of having run away from the tapping noise, thrust out his chest and said bravely, "Could I ride with you, Mr.

Kristinsson? I'm not afraid. Then I could bring the ponies back."

Olaf and Pete looked at Ricky in amazement.

"You want to sit on my lap?" the pilot asked, laughing. Then his look of amusement turned to one of serious thought. "We just might be able to do that. How much do you weigh?"

"Fifty-five pounds. And I've got muscles too."

Ricky flexed his biceps. Mr. Kristinsson felt the boy's arm. "Good. Courage and muscles are a fine combination."

It was decided that Ricky could sit on his lap. Their combined weight did not exceed the load limit. The safety belt could be strapped around both of them. Together they would fly off in search of the pony thief.

"We'll walk along and try to catch up," Pete said. "Crickets! What I wouldn't give for a ride like that!"

The older boys watched as Mr. Kristinsson took his seat and Ricky climbed into place. "Here, I have an extra pair of goggles," the pilot said and set them over Ricky's head. Then the engine was started and the rotor engaged, kicking up dust and bending the sparse grasses.

Ricky had a fluttery feeling in the pit of his stomach when the chopper swooped up off the ground and roared away at a furious speed. The rocks, black lava and patches of grass blurred to his vision as the craft whizzed in the direction the pony thief had taken.

The boy opened his mouth to ask a question but the wind took his breath away. His heart pounded like the beat of the rotor. Everything tingled right down to his fingertips.

In a few minutes Mr. Kristinsson's hand touched his shoulder, then pointed ahead. Off in the distance, like tiny toys, rode a horseman leading three ponies. Soon the copter hovered over the thief, dropping lower and lower. The rider gazed up fearfully. Ricky recognized him at once—the same fellow he had seen in Shoreham and at Keflavik!

The copter swooped a few yards over the villain, who dropped the halter of the lead pony, bent his head down, whipped his horse and galloped away as fast as he could.

Mr. Kristinsson chased him for a minute, then circled back to the ponies. They had reared and run a distance, but now stood in a frightened huddle.

The chopper landed far enough away from the animals as not to scare them again. When Ricky stepped out, his knees were shaking a little. He drew a deep breath and grinned at the pilot. "Boy, oh boy, that was some ride!"

"Are you all right?" Mr. Kristinsson asked.

"Sure. I've seen that guy before too." Ricky told what he knew about the pony thief.

The pilot was amazed to hear this. "Sounds as if this fellow has it in for you Hollisters. Well, you'd better hurry back with the ponies now, Ricky."

The beasts were tied one to the other and the boy mounted the lead animal.

"By the way," Mr. Kristinsson added with a smile, "why don't you keep those goggles? They look very good on you."

"Thanks." Ricky grinned and turned the ponies around. Then he started back along the trail. The copter roared up into the air then zoomed out of sight.

The redhead felt like a Norse hero returning from battle with the booty of conquest. He had watched the landmarks on their trek up the mountain and found his way easily. After a while he noticed Pete and Olaf coming toward him.

"Here are your ponies," Ricky said.

"You were great!" Olaf praised as they started homeward. Questions shot back and forth, and Ricky told of his fabulous flight. They had gone more than halfway when they saw the helicopter again. The chopper was on the ground and two men stood beside it.

As the boys drew closer, they saw that the pilot was guarding the other fellow, whose hands were tied behind his back.

"He caught him!" Ricky shouted.

"Here are your ponies!" Ricky said.

The ponies galloped to the scene and the boys fairly threw themselves out of the saddles.

"How did you do it? How did you catch him?" asked Pete.

Mr. Kristinsson said he had buzzed the fugitive again and again. "His horse became frightened and threw him off. He was stunned and I tied him up. I've already radioed the police. They'll be here any minute."

The prisoner looked surly and mumbled something when he saw the boys. He would not answer any of their eager questions however. Finally Mr. Kristinsson said, "You'd better go now. It is getting pretty late."

They started off again and soon passed a Land-Rover with two policemen heading toward the helicopter.

"I wonder what they'll find out about that crook," Olaf mused.

When the trio trotted up to the farm and unsaddled the ponies, their parents and the girls hastened over to the stable to find what had kept them so long. They were startled to learn what had happened.

"Congratulations," Mr. Sveinsson said. "So you caught one of those rascals. I just hope we can round up the others too."

"Someone's waiting for you inside," Mr. Hollister said.

The boys did not know what to expect. As they walked from the barn to the house, Holly chatted all the way. She told the story of how the big policeman chased her from underneath the bandstand because the President of Iceland was going to speak.

"Yikes!" Ricky said. "Did you see the President?"

Holly nodded. "He hugged me."

By this time they were in the living room, where a tall man with a broad face and huge hands greeted them. He was introduced as Lieutenant Gunnarsson of the Icelandic police. He smiled at the boys and took a seat.

"I have come to hear your story, to get all the parts of the strange puzzle and see if I can fit them together." He looked into the faces of each of the children and went on, "Now start at the beginning and tell me exactly how this mystery developed."

Pam began with Gram's Braille letter asking them to come to Froston to meet Helga. Then Holly told about the stranger who tried to get the sailplane model in Shoreham. The detective listened intently, taking notes as the mystery deepened— the near accident with the sailplane—the troll by the side of the road late at night on the way to Gram's house, finding the troll hat, the burglary at the Petersons', the cutoff of power and the strange footprints.

Lieutenant Gunnarsson rolled his eyes at the clue of the Icelandic candy wrapper. "Hm," he said, "excellent detective work."

He jotted down more notes about the theft of the sailplane crates, the prowlers, and finally the episode at the ski lodge.

"I will go back there tomorrow to investigate." He looked at the older boys. "Do you want to come with me?"

"Oh yes, certainly," Pete and Olaf replied.

"I'd like to go too," Pam spoke up.

Lieutenant Gunnarsson nodded. "Fine."

Holly, Helga, Ricky and Sue wanted to join him, also, but their mothers objected. "Too many detectives spoil the broth," Mrs. Hollister said with a smile.

About ten o'clock the next morning, Lieutenant Gunnarsson arrived with two Land-Rovers and four policemen. The three children hopped in and all started off for the suspicious ski lodge.

After threading carefully through the boulder-strewn foothills, the vehicles started up toward the place where the boys had tied their ponies. There the cars were parked and everyone got out.

The lieutenant signaled to them. "We must go quietly," he warned. "The thieves might have a permanent lookout here."

Pete and Olaf nodded and led the way, climbing nimbly up the hillside.

Suddenly Pam cried out a shrill warning. The boys glanced up. A large boulder was rolling toward them!

It bounced, gathered speed, and headed directly at Pete Hollister!

CHAPTER 17

The Thingvellir Spy

For a split second Pete stared at the boulder bouncing down at him. As it veered to the left, he dived in the opposite direction. The sharp stones dug into his arms and legs, but the huge rock sailed past inches from his body.

Pete sat up shakily and watched the boulder hurtling into the wide open spaces below.

The others rushed up. "Are you okay, son?" asked Lieutenant Gunnarsson anxiously.

"Just scratched up a bit," Pete replied. "You know, I think somebody shoved that stone down on purpose."

The detective nodded in agreement and all set up the hill again. When they were fifty feet from the ski lodge, two men burst out the door. They scrambled along a stony ridge toward a couple of horses tethered together to a chunk of lava.

"Halt!" shouted Lieutenant Gunnarsson, but they did not stop.

One of them turned to glance over his shoulder.

He tripped and fell headlong. Before he could rise, Pete and Olaf streaked ahead and leaped on top of him.

After a fierce struggle, the gasping fugitive lay prone. Pete had one arm twisted behind his back, Olaf the other.

A policeman hauled the prisoner to his feet and handcuffed him, while the others chased the second fellow. He reached his horse, however, flung himself into the saddle and escaped down the mountain.

"Take a Land-Rover! Get him!" roared the lieutenant, and two of his men dashed off.

The captured suspect looked sullen and glared at the boys as Lieutenant Gunnarsson searched him for identification. "So. I've heard of this one. He has a bad record. A well-educated man too. What a pity," the officer said. "Well, let's search the ski lodge."

The two policemen stayed with the prisoner and the lieutenant entered the building with the children.

"Somebody has been living here all right," Pam observed, looking around in the large, barren lobby. Embers were still glowing in the fireplace. Empty food cans were strewn about and a half-eaten loaf of bread lay on a table.

"It puzzles me," said Lieutenant Gunnarsson,

"why these fellows were hiding out here. I'd say there were much better places in town."

"Could they have been searching for the varda with the silver coins in it?" Olaf asked.

"But how would they know about that?" the officer asked. "Well," he added, "we'd better check this place for clues."

But although they investigated every nook and cranny of the building, nothing unusual turned up.

After a while, Pete wandered outdoors.

"Where are you going?" Pam asked and followed him.

"I've got a hunch," Pete said and stopped at the place where the prisoner had stumbled and fallen. "Maybe he dropped something." He searched the area carefully, moving every small stone.

Pam helped him. They walked in ever-widening circles, bending down so as not to miss even a shred of evidence.

"What's this?" Pam said suddenly. She picked up something brown that looked like a twig and showed it to Pete.

"It's rolled paper, like a parchment!" They hastened back to the ski lodge just as the two policemen came back to report that the second suspect had gotten away.

"We found something!" Pete said and handed the tiny scroll to the lieutenant, who spread it out carefully. On it were small characters written in ancient Gothic script.

"It's very old," the officer said, "and I can't read it. It would take a scholar to translate these symbols."

"May we keep it?" asked Pam.

"Sure, why not? If we need it we'll let you know."

All the while, Pete had carefully watched the eyes of the prisoner. They seemed to be glued to the parchment.

"He knows what it is," the boy thought. "And it must be important too."

Then the officers marched their man down the hill and the children followed.

"You take our friend here to headquarters. We'll interrogate him later," Lieutenant Gunnarsson told one of his men. "I'll drive the children home first."

Minutes later they were on their way.

"I wonder who can read Gothic script," Pete mused.

"My mother can," Olaf remarked and said that Mrs. Sveinsson had translated some old manuscripts for the National Museum.

"Then she can read what's on this parchment!" Pete exclaimed. He could hardly wait to get back. What if there was a secret message concealed in the strange note he held in his hand?

When they reached the Sveinsson farm, they waved good-by to Lieutenant Gunnarsson and hastened into the house. The women were chatting in the living room, where the younger children worked on a puzzle on the floor.

Pete was so excited that he nearly tripped over them as he hurried to show their hostess the piece of parchment. "Will you please tell us what it says, Mrs. Sveinsson?" he asked.

The woman rose, went to a desk and pulled out a large magnifying glass. Then she spread the scroll on the table.

"It's very, very old," she said. "Where did you find it?"

Olaf told her.

"It looks as if it may have been hidden in a varda," Mrs. Sveinsson went on.

Pete snapped his fingers. "I had a hunch those crooks dug up something!" he said. "Olaf, I'll bet that fellow threw it away before he was captured so the police wouldn't get it!"

Mrs. Sveinsson studied the message intently. Pam pressed close to her and looked over her shoulder.

"Is it a secret message?" she asked hopefully.

"Seems to me it's a little verse," said Mrs. Sveinsson and read slowly:

"The silver bag you won't find here,
   It's safely hid in Thingvellir."

Pam shivered with excitement. "The silver bag of old coins!" she cried. "It's a clue to where it is hidden!"

"But where is thingamajig?" Ricky wanted to know.

Olaf grinned. "Thingvellir, you mean? That's a famous place. The first parliament in the world, called the *Althing*, assembled there."

Ricky looked lost and Mrs. Sveinsson explained it in simple terms. "In the ancient days of Iceland the chieftains met there once a year. They made laws and decided how best to protect themselves."

"It was like a grand holiday," Helga put in. "When the clans gathered they had fun and feasts and talked about all that had happened during the year."

"But Thingvellir is a large place," Olaf remarked. "It won't be easy to find the silver bag."

"I have an idea," Helga spoke up. "Maybe it's in the spot where the chieftains had their tents in the olden days?"

Her mother explained that some of the places were marked by stones set into the ground, but other campsites were not. She added, "But don't you think we should tell the museum about this first? Maybe they'd like to join in the search."

"Not yet, Mother!" Helga pleaded. "Give us a chance to look for it before anybody else. We might find the bag of coins ourselves!"

Mrs. Sveinsson thought for a moment. "All right. I'll drive you there after lunch."

In less than an hour the station wagon was

filled with excited children, as their mothers drove them toward Thingvellir. The road crossed a barren plain, lined with outcroppings of jagged purplish rocks.

Mrs. Sveinsson finally turned into a side road and parked the car on top of a winding cliff. Everyone got out. Below them stretched a vast lake, fed by a swift-flowing river. Directly beneath the craggy cliff was the green roof of a large restaurant.

"Off to the left," Mrs. Sveinsson pointed, "is the hillside where the chieftains met. Go ahead and find your treasure. I'll follow you."

A steep, bumpy trail led down past a rocky gully where Olaf said the ancient Norsemen kept their horses during the Althing session.

"A natural corral," Pete observed. "See? A couple of ponies are in there now."

Mrs. Hollister decided to go back into the car with Sue, because a chill wind had made the little girl begin to shiver. They turned on the radio, but their attention was diverted by a motorcycle that pulled up and parked behind them.

A goggled man got off, walked to the edge of the cliff and stared down at the children, who by this time had reached the old campsite.

Helga and Pam knelt side by side, feeling under stones. Ricky and Holly were roaming around like ground squirrels, glancing into every crevice in the rugged ground.

The cyclist climbed down and trailed behind them. Mrs. Hollister honked the horn a couple of times, but because of the strong wind, Pete was the only one to notice the faint signal. He glanced around and saw the man staring but the fellow turned suddenly as if to look at the lake. After a while, however, his eyes drifted back to the searchers.

Pete nudged Olaf.

"Something wrong?" the Icelander asked.

"I think we're being spied on," Pete replied. "Doesn't that guy look familiar?"

Olaf turned around. "I'll say!" he whispered excitedly. "He's the one who got away at the ski lodge! He must have been able to figure out what was in that old scroll!"

"And now he realizes we know the secret too!"

"What'll we do?"

"Let's walk over to the girls," Pete suggested. "I have a plan."

When they reached Pam and Helga, Pete spoke to them in a low voice. Then the girls slowly moved some distance away and began to act out the part they were to play.

Helga dropped to her knees and felt a clump of grass. Putting her hand beneath it, she suddenly cried out, "I found it! I found the silver bag!"

The spy reacted instantly. He leaped over the rocky ground, crying, "Give it to me! That's mine!"

"I found the silver bag!" Helga cried.

"No. You can't have it!" Helga said bravely holding her hands behind her back as if she were hiding something. But nothing was there but her ten fingers!

Still the fellow advanced menacingly and Pete and Olaf went into action. They raced over and jumped on the man's back. All three tumbled to the damp ground in a tangle of hands and feet.

In addition, Pam called out to Mrs. Sveinsson. With a shout, she, too, launched into the fray.

The poor spy had as much chance as a snowball in the midnight sun. Mrs. Sveinsson and the boys pinned him quickly. Olaf ripped off his belt, as did Pete. They bound the stranger hand and foot.

When the man found that he had been caught by a ruse, he struggled and shouted, but it did him no good.

Olaf cupped his hands and called down to the restaurant for assistance. Two men hastened up. Upon hearing the story, they loosened the captive's ankles, tied his arms securely and marched him down the hill to await the police.

On the way back home, Mrs. Sveinsson said, "The silver bag may never be found, but at least you caught another one of the gang!"

Her home quivered with excitement that evening. Lieutenant Gunnarsson arrived later to say that the man caught at Thingvellir was a former sailor known as a troublemaker. He thanked the young detectives for their clever trick, and then suggested that they turn the ancient parchment over to the National Museum.

The children agreed that the government might do a better job of hunting for the treasure. Besides, the sailplane championship would take place the next day and they all wanted to watch it.

After the officer left, supper was served and an hour later the children trooped off to bed. Finally the guesthouse grew still.

Pam listened to the quiet for a long time before drifting off into a light sleep. She turned restlessly. All at once, she sat up, wide awake. Her watch said it was midnight. Had she heard a noise or was it in her dream?

She crept out of bed and quickly went to the window. Suddenly she flung a hand against her mouth so as not to cry out in fright at what she saw.

Outside stood two trolls and a skeleton! One of the little men pointed to the door and beckoned to Pam.

"Helga!" she cried in a quavering voice. "The trolls are here!"

"What?" Helga jumped up groggily.

Then the girls felt their way to the hall and called Pete and Olaf.

The older boys hastened downstairs with Ricky

at their heels. Excitedly Pam told what had happened.

Taking a deep breath, Pete opened the door. There stood the trolls. They did not run away! Instead, one of them spoke in Icelandic, *"Viltu gjera svo vel og hleypa mēr okkur inn?"*

CHAPTER 18

A Spooky Catch

"Wh—what did he say?" Pam asked Helga.

"He said, 'Please let me in.'"

"Yes, they want to come inside," Olaf whispered.

Amazed, the children stood in the doorway and stared. Two trolls wore green pants, red jackets and pointed hats. The third was dressed in a skeleton costume, which looked even more eerie when the moon broke from behind a bank of clouds.

Now the gaping youngsters could see better. Suddenly Holly cried out, "Oh! They're not trolls at all. I know that one!" She pointed to the smallest. "He's the midget from the silver shop!"

"Please let us in," the little fellow said again, this time in English. "It's important. We are here to warn you of the thieves."

His voice sounded urgent and sincere. Olaf motioned for them to enter and reached out for the light switch, but the trolls begged him not to turn it on.

175

"Who are you?" Pete asked. "What is this all about?"

The shortest one said he was Kari, the silversmith. The others were his friends Einar and Rasn.

"We must hurry," Kari said, "if we are to catch the thief."

Olaf and Helga spoke rapidly to the midgets in smooth, softly flowing Icelandic.

"What are you saying?" Sue begged.

"Shh, not now," Helga whispered. "Come. Follow me. And please be quiet."

"Bend down low," Olaf advised. "We don't want anybody to see us."

Helga crept quickly along the path toward the house. The darkness meant nothing to her. She knew every inch of the way. Following her came Olaf and the Hollisters. The midgets brought up the rear.

Helga went through the back door of the house. The others filed in quietly. It was chilly on their bare feet, and Holly started to sneeze. But she grabbed her nose and squinched up her face. The sneeze disappeared.

Olaf led everyone into the living room while Helga tiptoed upstairs.

Silence seemed to cover all of Iceland. If there was a thief lurking, he was as quiet as the clouds that scudded over the sleeping house.

In a few minutes Helga came down with Mr.

Sveinsson and Mr. Hollister. Pete glanced at the glowing numerals of his wrist watch. It was twelve midnight.

Suddenly a small noise brought everybody alert. A dark form was climbing through the dining room window. The figure stopped, listened, put one foot on the carpet.

Then it happened. The house lights flashed on. At the same time the fathers seized the most frightened burglar in the world! His face paled and his hands trembled like Jell-O. "I—I give up. Oh, those kids!" He closed his eyes as to blot out the view of the young detectives. Then he was bound to a chair with ropes to await the police.

The mothers came down from upstairs with blankets to put around the children.

"Now for some explanations," Mr. Sveinsson said sternly, looking at the midgets.

"We were sorry we had to scare you," Kari said to the children, "and we apologize. You see, the whole thing started when my friends and I flew to Montreal on our vacation. On the way we sat behind two men."

"They didn't notice us," Einar said.

"And they were plotting a robbery," Kari went on. "We heard one say, 'Once we get the invention we can sell it for a million.' They also mentioned a collection of filigree silver jewelry and talked about their haul in the woods."

"I give up. Oh, those kids!"

"So we went to the police as soon as we arrived in Montreal," Rasn said. "But they laughed at us!"

"Well, it was true we couldn't prove anything," Kari said, "and we didn't even know where that place in the woods was."

"Uncle Sig's cottage in Froston, I'll bet!" Olaf put in.

Einar bobbed his head. "Anyway, the police told us to run along and leave the detective work to them."

"So we decided to catch the robbers ourselves!" Kari went on and told that they had followed the pair on another flight to Froston. "We stayed at the same motel and spied on them. When they prowled around the Petersons' cottage at night, we scared them away!"

"You almost scared us away too," Pam said. "Why did you do that?"

Kari replied, "We knew the bad men were around and wanted you safely in the house at night. That's why we poked you and rewound your tape recorder."

"And while we did, the crooks ransacked the house," Einar added sadly.

Pete shook his head. "I wish we had stayed home that night."

"We came up with a clue, though," Kari went on. "We overheard the crooks say that since the stuff wasn't there, it must be at their relatives' house in Reykjavik."

"So you followed them right back to Iceland?" Holly asked.

"Yes. We spied on them as much as we could in our free time and found out their target was the Sveinsson house. But we didn't know when they would break in, so we came around every night dressed up as trolls and scared them again."

"Tonight we saw a pony tied not too far from here," Rasn said. "So we figured that at least one of the crooks was hiding out to survey the house." He explained that they didn't want the lights to be turned on, so they came to the guesthouse, hoping the children would be secretive.

Holly giggled. "We were," and twirled a pigtail.

"Actually," Pete said. "Three of the crooks were already caught."

"Oh. We didn't know," Kari said. "Then the whole gang is rounded up now."

Just then headlights shone down the road and Lieutenant Gunnarsson drove up with another officer. Quickly he was introduced to the midgets and heard their story. He turned to the prisoner, who was surprised that the police knew his name and background.

"Your pals talked," the lieutenant said, "and I think we have this case solved now." He said that the gang had come across the information that Mr. Peterson had the sailplane invention and planned to steal it. In eavesdropping at the Sveinssons, they had also learned of the filigree collections owned by the sisters.

"One of the crooks went to Shoreham since he suspected the model contained the invention," Gunnarsson explained, "but had no luck. Two others flew to Canada for the double haul."

When they failed both in Canada and Shoreham, they intercepted the sailplane crates, hoping the new invention had already been installed on Mr. Hollister's craft.

"That's why one of the crates was open!" Mr. Hollister said.

"Yes. When they didn't find the invention, they followed the children hoping to pick up a clue. At the museum they learned of the secret in the varda." The officer chuckled. "These crooks were greedy. If they hadn't bothered to look for the ancient varda and hid out in the ski lodge, they might still have their freedom."

"I doubt it," Mr. Sveinsson said. "Not with the Hollisters in Iceland."

Lieutenant Gunnarsson said to Kari, "I still would have preferred it if you had come to us with your information."

"We started to enjoy playing detectives," the midget replied.

"Everybody seems to like it," Lieutenant Gunnarsson said with a wink at the children. Then the officer left with the prisoner.

The next day bustled with excitement. The championship meet was on, and the weather was perfect for the event.

Crowds of people milled about the edge of the green airstrip as the sailplanes, one after another, soared silently into the sky.

The youngsters cheered as Mr. Sveinsson's plane nosed up into the deep blue, and when Mr. Hollister soared off, his children clapped and shouted.

The wait seemed like forever, but then the beautiful silent birds floated down to earth once more. The officials busied themselves checking their electronic timers and examining the instrument panels of the sailplanes.

Mr. Sveinsson was declared the winner. He had stayed aloft longer than anyone else. But Mr. Hollister got a prize too. His altimeter showed that he had gone up the highest.

The spectators cheered as trophies were presented. Even the midgets, who had taken the day off, ran up to shake hands with the winners.

At home that evening everyone was in a gay and jolly mood. The trophies—small sailplanes mounted on silver globes—were set on the fireplace mantel and shone in the glow of the flickering hearth.

Sue lay on the floor, her chin cupped in her chubby hands. "All this time in Iceland," she said, "and I haven't seen a single muffin bird yet."

Helga rose quietly and went upstairs. She returned with a stuffed bird mounted on a chunk of lava.

"Here's your puffin," Helga said.